Dancing in Winter

and other stories

Edith Gallagher Boyd

ISBN: 978-1-731-29210-0

Dedicated to my Uncle, Father Joe Maguire

TABLE OF CONTENTS

ACKNOWLEDGMENTS

Many thanks to my editors

Joanne Gilmore

Katie Langan

Mary Rose O'Neill

Fran Martini

Margaret Spraitzar.

i

DOUBLE DODGING

The ball swished through the basket. Not only was it a buzzer beater, it was against one of our biggest rivals. My shot gave us the win against Whitaker High. The only casualty was my ankle blowing up like a melon - a crooked landing after a jump shot.

My dad often reminded me to tape my ankles, something about his being weak, but I couldn't take us to State worrying about injuries. Feeling a lot of pain, I made my way to the trainer's office and admitted my ankle needed help.

Luckily, the nurses' office at Springfield High was at the end of the hall close to the gym. They had all our records, and were nicer to us guys than the trainers. It was a Friday afternoon game, and the nurses were still on the job.

Joe, the trainer, wheeled me down to the nursing office and left me in the hall.

"Dylan, they'll take good care of you," he said.

Joe left me in the hall. I didn't want to be a big baby and call for the nurses, so I jut sat there. I heard one of the nurses whisper something about the medical records, and the State College student nurse said "He doesn't know?" In that question- like way girls end sentences with.

Mrs. Turner, the head nurse from forever, jumped a little when she saw me sitting there. "Joe said...Oh Dylan, I thought we were supposed to go get you. How's that ankle, honey?"

"It needs you, Mrs. Turner," I said, knowing I was one of her favorites.

1

"Yeah, yeah, yeah, Dylan. Save your lines for the girls...maybe our new student nurse, Ashley?" Careful not to say I thought Ashley was hot, I asked Mrs. Turner if Ashley was talking about me...the 'He doesn't know?'

I couldn't see Mrs. Turner's face behind me as she pushed my wheelchair to the infirmary, but I smelled a bull's eye, and started to get an uneasy feeling. She couldn't even come up with one of her jokes. She just cleared her throat and asked me to describe how I hurt my ankle.

After icing it, wrapping it, and putting my foot in a boot, Mrs. Turner called my mom and asked permission to give me two Tylenol. Like they were going to do anything. My buddy Matt would probably drive me to the victory party, where there'd be something stronger to help with the pain.

I didn't think I was dying or anything, hearing that talk in the nurses' office, or I wouldn't have made the varsity. But, it wasn't the first time people got quiet and nervous when I came on the scene. Memories of Aunt Barb with a little too much of dad's eggnog saying, "Marcie, you haven't told him . . . It's just wrong!" And then she got all red-faced when she saw me fixing a broken light on the Christmas tree.

Now that I would be sitting on the bench for most of the season, I had time to find out what it was I didn't know about myself. I should probably start with my parents, but my dad was so protective of my mom, he made me feel rotten if I said the wrong thing around her.

"Dylan, your mother has a headache. Dylan, turn down that music."

It was like we all revolved around what wasn't good for my mom.

But nothing made me feel worse than making her sad, so I tried not to.

Matt sent me a text that he would pick me up for the party. He didn't even make me ask. His truck was really old, so I made sure I had some cash for a cab to get us home if need be. I was waiting for the rumble of his F150, when my mother came up and hugged me from behind.

"I'm proud of you, Dylan. Know how hard it's going to be sitting on the bench, and you haven't complained once."

2

"Won't do me any good," I said, embarrassed by the catch in my voice.

"Dylan, if Matt or anybody else is drinking at the party, I'm a text or call away."

"Mom, I look dumb enough with this thing on my foot. All I need is Mommy picking me up.

"Sorry, Mom," I said, and turned around and gave her a real hug, a kindergarten type hug, until I heard Matt's truck sputtering up our street.

"They're sure it's just a sprain?" She said, as I pushed through the door,.

"Yeah, Mom. Mrs. Turner knows her stuff."

Matt looked at my booted foot and didn't say anything. We'd been friends since first grade, and he knew I didn't want to talk about it.

"Did you hear Billy's parents are out of town?" Matt said. "I helped him unload the keg. Billy said everybody can crash there."

Billy's house was perfect for a party - far out of town on acres of land. As Matt and I pulled into the muddy parking area, we could hear the music blasting from the house. I could already taste the shots going down my throat into my throbbing foot.

About to park, Matt reversed and dumped me at the front door, and then went to find a parking spot. Times like that, he was like the brother I always wanted.

When I hobbled into the party, everybody cheered, hooted and clapped about our victory over Whitaker.

"Tough break Dylan"

"But your shot was awesome!"

"How long you laid up?'

"Not sure."

Billy brought over a tray of shots to me and Matt. I grabbed one and loved the burning feeling in my throat, the hot, bitter pain relief. I noticed Matt with his hand up, not taking one from Billy.

"What's up, man? You helped with the keg," I said.

"I said I'd drive you. Here and home. Done deal."

Then, feeling like a wuss he said. "No way I'm gonna tangle with your mom, Dylan."

Whew, I thought. Even my buddies knew how my mom's focus was totally on me. Why couldn't she be in a bowling league or book club like other moms?

I hadn't kicked the weird feeling I had when I heard Ashley talking about me in the office.
It was kind of strange that just as I thought that, I saw her in a group of the older kids - friends of Billy's brother Roger .They were doing shots and getting pretty wasted.

" Springfield rules!"

"Whitaker sucks!"

It was like everybody there saw the game. It made me feel good re-living the jumper that put us ahead by one, just enough to beat those dickheads. A lot of the kids from Whitaker were rich and obnoxious, and they were used to winning.

When Billy walked by with another tray of shots, I took one and headed over to talk to Ashley, before I lost my nerve.

She had that glazed-eye look of somebody getting wasted, so I felt safer talking to an older, pretty girl. Somebody said she was hooked up with Billy's older brother, but he wasn't near her, so I took my shot.

"I'm Dylan," I said, pointing to my foot.

She leaned into me not flirty like...just nice like.

"Hurt a lot?"

"Nah," I said.

"What did you mean, 'He doesn't know?' That you asked Mrs. Turner?"

"Don't know what you're talking about," she said, looking down.

Billy's brother Roger yelled over, "Kid bothering you, Ash?" And I felt like decking him, but knew enough to just limp away over to my own friends. I found an empty spot on a couch and rested my leg on a coffee table.

From the angle I was sitting, I saw a pick-up game of b ball out back and that hurt worse than my foot. I was going to hate the bench. Matt shot a jumper that was awesome. He was cut before the season, and had been practicing every day. I owed him, and was determined to talk to Coach about giving him another shot at making the squad. Maybe now that I was out, Coach would give him a second look.

Billy came over with another tray of shots and I thought how pissed his parents would be when they found out about the party. Mr. Marshall was a big shot in the local police department. The pain in my ankle was bumming me out, and I just felt like going home.

All of a sudden, Mr. Marshall burst through the front door and started yelling "Shut that god damned thing off! pointing to the music. Roger, Billy...get these kids out of here!'

Mrs. Marshall looked like somebody died, and went to Billy's dad, trying to calm him down. Both Billy and Roger were scared shitless.

After a lot of yelling and cursing, Mr. Marshall called Uber for the kids to get home.

Billy's mom took over ordering a few group rides and made a shushing face to her husband. I imagined Billy and his brother would be grounded for at least a month.

Ashley walked away from Roger and the older kids and plopped down on the couch next to me. She looked pretty shot ....and not so pretty.. and whispered, "Your parents...Ask your parents.' She got up and walked that way trashed people do.. right out the front door to the Uber van.

Hoping Matt and I could sneak out of the party, I was ready to make my mother tell me what the big deal was, but remembered she would smell the alcohol on me, and it was best to wait. I watched Matt go over to Mr. Marshall and talk to him.

Billy said way loud, "I swear on Mom, he's telling the truth. He didn't drink. He's driving Dylan who got hurt in the win today." By the time I got over there to Matt, Mr. Marshall wasn't as mad and congratulated me on the buzzer beating shot.

When Matt dropped me off at home, I heard Mom and Aunt Barb shouting. It sounded like they'd been drinking too. I decided to wait in the side yard. My dad was acting like a ref, "Marcie, Barb...calm down."

"Tom, Marcie is selfish. She's just selfish to keep it from him."

"Easy for you to say. You popped out babies like a bunny rabbit."

5

And then my mother started to cry...a big wailing sound and it made my chest hurt and it scared me, too. My parents never made a scene. I felt like telling Aunt Barb off, but knew I was wasted, although old man Marshall sobered me up a lot with his fit.

I thought of texting Matt and asking him to come get me, but felt like I needed to help mom stop crying. As I was about to go inside, I heard the screen door shut and my dad on the phone with Uncle Ralph.

"They're at it again, Ralph. Can you pick Barb up, or do you want me to take her home?" "Thanks, Ralph. I'll see you in a few."

Then Dad was quiet and said. "Don't worry. They'll be on the phone tomorrow...and the next day. You know how it goes."

Dad went back inside and I decided to sit on the bench under our maple tree out back.

It's amazing how little I felt the throb in my ankle with all the crazy shit that happened tonight. Grown ups wigging out, Billy getting caught, my mom drunk and a mess. And I put the pieces of the puzzle together that had been there all along. Stuff I knew, but didn't want to know. Things I heard way before Aunt Barb's eggnog rant to Mom. That I was adopted, and there was a lady out there who gave me away.

I couldn't hear my parents, but trusted my dad to calm my mom down. I sucked in my breath at the thought that she wasn't really my mom, but then felt guilty, cause she was. Who else would have stuck up for me when Miss Perkins had a pick on me in second grade? Who else coated my skin when I had poison ivy or chicken pox? I felt the tears coming, so glad I was alone. Why would my mom keep this from me? I saw After School Specials where the adoptive parents sit the kids down to tell them they got them in a special way. Those shows were kind of sappy, but that's how it was supposed to be done.

Why the lying, and who was the woman who didn't want me?

After I rubbed my eyes with my sleeve and calmed down, I went inside and sat across from my parents. Dad's arm was around Mom on the couch. She was leaning into him and still hiccupping, but I wouldn't go over to her, even though it was killing me to see her so upset.

"I figured it out. I'm not your kid. I'm somebody else's who didn't want me" and I started to cry. Really sob like maybe never in my life. Both of them came over to me but I pushed them away and yelled "Liars! You're nothing but liars Why keep it from me? "

I knew I'd be grounded a lot longer than Billy Marshall for talking to my parents like that, but I didn't care. Since the ceiling didn't fall down on me, I pushed it further and walked into the kitchen and grabbed one of my dad's beers, opened it, and took a swig.

"Dylan," my dad said looking as mad as Mr. Marshall. I felt relieved that everything wasn't upside down. I put down the beer.

"Your mother and I," he began.

My mother said, "No Tom. I need to speak for myself."

"I needed to believe I gave you life. I resented the experts who tried to take this from me. The ones who said I needed to let you know you were adopted."

Dad jumped in. "Mom and I never wanted to hurt you, and were preparing to tell you on your birthday when all the records open. "

"Your father wanted that. I would have found a way to stop it," my mom said, still hiccupping, but showing the kind of guts Coach was constantly preaching.

"Who is she? The one who had me?"

My parents kept interrupting each other saying that tomorrow would be better to talk. I believed them that they were done with the lying and hiding. It was late, and my mother rarely drank, and I was still a little wasted, but I told them I probably wouldn't sleep unless they told me more.

"Dad," I said when my voice was almost normal, "you always say, 'There's no time like the present' " making my voice catch a little.

"Dylan," my mother said, "Your birth mother didn't want to give you up for adoption. She wanted to re unite with you when you came of age. Megan was a teenager, and felt unable to care for you. Honey, she was just a kid."

"Mom, can I meet her after my birthday?"

My parents gave each other a really long look.

"What is it,?" I said.

My dad came to me, and brought me over to sit between them on the couch, and I didn't fight him. I leaned back into the couch and rested my booted foot on the coffee table.

"Megan, your birth mother, died in a car accident before you were a year old," my dad said." Our lawyer let us know after it happened."

"I'm so sorry, Dylan," my parents said together.

It was so much to take in. Now that they actually admitted it, what I suspected all along was real. And I would never meet her, and see what she was like, or get a chance to yell at her for giving me away. And good stuff, too. Like seeing if I looked like her, or maybe if we could be friends some day. Or ask her about my other father.

I was done crying for the night, and said the craziest thing to my dad.

"Why the bullshit about weak ankles when we're not even related?"

I regretted it as soon as I said it, especially when he sucked in his breath like he was shot. He made me look at him and said, "We love you, son. We forget, sometimes how you came into our lives. If you believe nothing else about us, believe that."

And I did.

"There's more to tell you, Dylan," my mom said.

Uh oh, I thought, Started thinking waiting until tomorrow was not a bad idea.

"When Megan gave birth to you, you had a twin brother.'

"Is he dead, too?"

"There are things we are legally bound to resist, until you are eighteen, but the agency did reveal recently, he's a healthy young man who goes to Spaulding High in Monroe County. We wanted you both, but he was already taken when we were approved."

"What's his name?"

"Andrew. Andy Kowalski."

Andy. I had a brother named Andy. I rolled the name around in my head, and wondered if he knew about me or if the stupid agency rules made him clueless, too.

The next few days with my parents were pretty strange, but I couldn't hold onto the piss I had for them. My friends were always telling me how cool it was that my parents remembered their names and really listened to them, and made them feel important.

I hated that I would never know my first mother, but I agreed to wait to go see Andy until after my birthday. I knew Matt would take me. When I told him the whole story, he just nodded and didn't say anything stupid...He didn't say much of anything at all.

On my eighteenth birthday, I was still limping around, and asked my mom to pick the restaurant for our family to celebrate together. Felt I owed her for stepping up, not just now, but from the beginning. If she promised to whisper, I agreed that she could say what she always said before I blew out my candles. "Who's my best boy?"

When Matt's F 150 rolled into Spaulding High, I was excited, but scared. Would he look like me? Would he be chill like Matt? We could hear the crowds roaring for the b ball game. The game had already started.

It was hard to find a seat so we had to go up to the nose bleed section.

Matt saw him first. He elbowed me and said, "Shit, Dylan. It's like I'm seeing double. He hits his chest three times when he leaves the bench."

I can't describe how it felt to see this guy who could have been me...the way he faked left, the way he took his jumpers, and his face was like looking in the mirror.

I had to look away. I couldn't talk.

I shot a glance at Matt, and he had that pasty far away look he had after his dad left home.

"Dylan," he said quietly. "It will be so cool to get a brother."

"Another brother, Matt. Met my first one in first grade."

He looked sideways, and smiled.

We each snapped some photos of Andy, before we left.

I poked him and said, "Let's go see Coach."

"Yeah," he said, with the kind of spunk Coach liked.

We made our way down the bleachers to his F-150, and headed for home.

From: Adelaide Magazine

THE GRAVERS LANE LOCAL

The job in the city was working out for me. Actually, the job
wasn't great, but the apartment I chose, and the train I rode to work
were fun. Each had separated me from a bad trend I had leaned
into; getting wasted with my friends, complaining a lot, and
accomplishing little. The downward spiral my life had taken since
John's telling me he needed space. I needed a change of locale and
a straight job. Cooper Products offered me a generous salary, and
an opportunity to choose a small apartment of my own.

Nicole, my sister-in-law, helped me decorate my place with
her special flair. Not only was she artistic, she was a good bargain
hunter, so the finished decor didn't cost me a week's pay at Cooper.
She also tuned me into the Gravers Lane Local.

I began to enjoy the 8:10 A.M. Local, even though the 8:20
Express would get me into the city more quickly. It was
comforting to see regulars at the Stanton Street stop; a retired
couple walking with the self-satisfied gait of a strong portfolio, and
a dreamy young couple who boarded with the guy twirling his
fingers through the woman's cork-screw curls. Their bliss warmed
me more than my thermos of coffee. I imagined a long, happy
future for them.

My imagined dream for them began to inhabit a great deal of
my ride into the city. Perhaps it was to buffer me from the bland
emotional life at Cooper Products. Or to protect me from
reminiscing about John. I pictured the young woman, whom I
named Ginger, to wear a traditional lacy wedding dress, and for

her ardent suitor, Eddie, to be casually dressed, and for their nuptials to be an outdoorsy kind of thing.

When Ginger caught my eye, I hastily looked away, as I didn't want to meet them, and find their names or their lives to be normal or banal. Nicole began to worry about me. I was nearly friendless since I moved, and managed to insult my partying crowd. Nicole sat with me in my window seat, which she decorated, and clinked her wine glass to mine. " Beth, you seem obsessed with these people on the train," she said sincerely.

Had my interest in them become a pathology of sorts? I wasn't aware of the frequency of my tales of the train. For Nicole to assert this, I felt the need to venture into an evening class, or to join a book club, and get out of my head. I was careful to avoid speaking about my train people during the remainder of Nicole's visit. She was not only my decorator. She was also my first guest. The night Nicole referred to my train obsessions, I re-iterated how lucky my brother Joe was to have met and married her.

Later that evening, I opened my windows and heard the gentle thwack of a bat hitting a ball and calls of "little help" from the field behind my apartment. The ball field reminded me of our childhood home. Behind our home was a ball park, and as I settled into my new digs, I remembered playing Monopoly or Scrabble with Joe, on hot summer nights, with players' comments and cheers chanting a gentle chorus in the background.

As taken as I was with Ginger and Eddie, I began to develop an interest in others who passed through the portals of The Gravers Lane Local. There was the accountant whom I passed on the streets of the city, when the train reached its destination. I don't believe I imagined his occupation, as I saw him enter an accounting firm, briefcase in hand, no chit chat with the vendors on the street corners.

And a cardiologist and I struck up a few conversations on the Local, when we happened to land on the seat next to the other. I noticed his name tag under his tan cardigan, and asked him about his field. I remember the morning well… slightly chilly for early fall, when I worked up the nerve to say, "What kind of doctor are you?" He hesitated, and answered, "A good one," with a charming smile, then quickly became serious, and said, "A cardiologist. I work at City Hospital."

" Do you work in the city?" He said with an earnest tilt of his head. I could picture trusting him with my medical care, then shuddered that I would need it at my age.

"I work in marketing at Cooper Products" I replied, straightening my shoulders to look the part. He clearly didn't find my occupation intriguing, as he gave me a tepid smile and settled into his seat, and then, remembering his manners, he asked a few questions about my work.

I liked Dr. Baldwin, even though we had few further conversations during our morning commute. He was akin to a pillar of normalcy in my new life in my new neighborhood. We often just nodded to the other, after he boarded at the same stop as the well- heeled retirees. I didn't know the walking couple, but the strut was not that of a couple who had worked any graveyard shifts in hospitals or diners.

One crisp, fall morning, I was so taken with the orange and gold maples, that I almost missed Eddie alight from his seat, to greet Dr. Baldwin as he made his way down the aisle. A frisson of fear crept up me that I couldn't quite explain. Of course it was possible they were neighbors, or Eddie's dad was a golf buddy of the doc, but something primal in me told me that was not the case.

Somehow, the wedding with lilacs and ivy, or sand dunes and seascape, with Ginger ethereal in her beauty, seemed iffy to me, and I noticed my coffee thermos was no longer hot or even warm. Beth, get a hold of yourself, I said, in my best fatherly voice.....this day dreaming has gotten out of hand. My dad's pragmatism collided with my lifelong fondness for fantasy.

But my job was not inspiring, and the train trips so interesting, with the varied people and views whizzing by. The mesmerizing sounds of the train slowing for yet another stop, had become as soothing as the summer sounds of baseball when I first moved to my apartment. Who cared if Nicole thought I was becoming a bit unhinged?

I did, and I was very relieved when I received a message from my brother that he and Nicole were throwing a Halloween party. I hadn't been to a party since John and I were a couple, the thought of which sent a stab of pain right through me. I distracted myself by thinking about Ginger and Eddie.

Uh oh. Here it was again. The fantasies about the Gravers Lane Local. Easier on me than facing the extra twenty something pounds I was carrying around. I was avoiding my parents as they wouldn't say anything, but the arch of my mother's eyebrow would be enough to let me know how she saw me.

Unable to stick with Atkins or join Gold's Gym, I decided to dress as a witch or a dragon, something I could pull off without working off the weight. Not one of those sultry witches…I would be the old-fashioned kind, dreamed up to scare kids, for whatever reason some crazy person decided to scare kids. I considered asking Nicole to whip something together for me, but realized she would be busy decorating their home, and I sensed I may have become a bit of a pest, leaning on Nicole too frequently.

The invitation to the party sparked a resolve in me to begin walking and getting in shape. After the Local deposited me back home, I began to walk through my new neighborhood. I said good-bye to Ben & Jerry, and started to improve my diet. As I started to feel better about myself, I became less interested in Ginger and Eddie.

Or so I thought. A week before Joe and Nicole's party, I saw Dr. Baldwin approach Eddie at the Stanton Street Station. He grabbed Eddie's wrist, as if taking a pulse, and my heart clenched. Could Eddie be a patient? It certainly seemed that way. I couldn't ask Dr. Baldwin, and I didn't want to break the Eddie and Ginger spell to find they were Travis and Ashley. Nor could I express myself, yet again, to Nicole.

I threw myself into finding an attractive witch costume. My walks in the neighborhood and my climbing the steps at work had helped me shed some of the pounds that were plaguing me. I found a fun witch's outfit, complete with hat and wand.

While shopping for my outfit, I was surprised to hear Nicole's gentle voice asking if there was a stand alone scarecrow decoration. As I rounded out of my aisle into hers, She nearly shrieked,

"Beth, look at you, wasting away! You look great!" And then, she knitted her brow and said, "Are you O.K.? You're not sick or anything," …her voice trailing away.

"Ahh, thanks. No, I've been exercising and gave up ice cream. Does it really show?"

She placed a few things in her cart and hugged me tightly.

We stayed that way for a few seconds, and my throat caught, thinking of her support in the early post John dregs, withholding judgment of him or the situation. My heart, still enmeshed with his, didn't need criticism of him.

Appearing to read my thoughts, she said, "Joe has met some quality friends, Beth." Just as I was about to say something, I saw a familiar profile from the train. Ginger. She was to my left heading to the Pharmacy area of the Super Shop. I started to point her out to Nicole, and then remembered her concern, and told her how I was looking forward to the party, meaning it.

But preparing for the party didn't stop me from inching over near the Pharmacy and Ginger. But Nicole came back over to me to ask if I could go along that I didn't recognize Joe right away at the party, as he " has gone round the bend" about his costume.

Speaking softly, so as not to alert Ginger, I whispered, " I'll play along, but if there's anybody in the world I could pick out with a blindfold, it'd be Joe." I could say that to her without her becoming uncomfortable or possessive of Joe. From their first meeting, Nicole accepted the brother/sister bond between Joe and me.

And there were more than a few greeting cards I received from Joe, that I knew Nicole shopped for, and held the pen in his hand for him to sign.

The night of the party, I felt an excitement I hadn't felt in a while. I was getting fit, had reduced my drinking immensely, and was settling into my new apartment, which suited me so well. Look out guys, I thought as I applied the last bit of glitter around my eyes.

Joe and Nicole's place looked great with ghosts, witches and scarecrows lining the walkway, and orange and black streamers swaying with the ringing chimes Nicole placed on their back patio.

I noticed a guy dressed like Sherlock Holmes, and he noticed me. I could feel it.

I waved my wand around, and he smiled and walked over to me.

"You're Beth, Joe's sister," he said disarming me completely.

"Yes. I am. I consider it an honor," I said, hoping my glitter didn't accentuate my nose or make me look silly. "I've heard so much about you," he said, while guiding me over to the bar area set up for the occasion.

Although I preferred beer, I felt self-conscious ordering one, and settled for a vodka tonic. While stirring the little straw through my drink, looking down on the lime in it, I said, "You didn't tell me your name."

"Gerry.....Gerry Mc Laughlin," he said, with a glint in his eye that warmed me to him, and stirred feelings I hadn't felt in a while.

So this was Gerry. Joe had told me about him….all good things.

I slipped my drink slowly, remembering the excesses of my recent past, and asked him about himself. He only said a few things about himself before he glided me over to an empty couch, and asked me about our childhood, Joe's and mine. Unusual for a guy, I thought, to defer talk away from himself. A combination of my nerves, the vodka, and his warmth led to describing my new residence and the memories of past summers, with the thwack of baseballs, and parental curfews lifted. I felt relaxed enough to begin telling him about the Gravers Lane Local. And some of its inhabitants.

When Nicole drifted by us with her cell phone heading to the patio, I became silent and heard her say, "Dad, did you ask Dr. Baldwin?"

I nearly grabbed Gerry's pipe prop right out of his hand and said, "Did she say Dr. Baldwin?"

He looked at me warily and said, "Beth, what's the big deal if she did?" In the split second it takes to process stuff, I was pleased that Gerry appeared jealous, and fearful that I had truly gone nuts to react so strongly to the mention of Dr. Baldwin.

Leaving Gerry on the couch, I smiled and said I'd be right back. I followed behind Nicole and heard digitalis....one glass of red wine, and knew it had to do with her dad's heart issues.

Gerry managed to distract me, which bode well for a possible friendship, and maybe more between us. I fumbled with my i-phone when he asked for my contact information. I began to hope this could be a casual thing, that I could go on a few dates and wear those sling-back heels that sat in my closet. I wasn't crazy about the name Gerry, but liked everything else about him.

Joe, whose costume did actually fool me, took off his mask and came to talk to us on the couch. I was pleased he showed no protective brotherly concern about Gerry's attention to me. I excused myself and went into the kitchen to hang out with Nicole. After a little give and take about the party and Gerry, I asked about her father, without revealing my looking for clues about Dr. Baldwin. It didn't take long for Doc Baldwin's name to come up. As always, Nicole was open and without guile, and she knew I liked her dad and would be interested in details about him.

"Dr. Baldwin has a satellite office on Stanton Street, but his home base is City Hospital, where he does a lot of pro bono work."

The conversation I overheard was a routine update, father to daughter. I was relieved that her father was not in a health crisis, and tickled that my train pal was connected to our family.

And when Gerry and I met for a dinner the Wednesday after the party, I felt a joy and quickening I hadn't felt in a while.

Thursday morning, after our dinner date, I awakened with an odd sense of dread.
Trying to be my father's daughter, I tried to find a practical reason for my feelings. It didn't take long to admit it would be a long wait until next Friday's pay check, as I had squandered the last one, preparing for my date.

Although the Stanton Street stop didn't produce the regulars, I did notice Eddie and Dr. Baldwin on the 5:20 Local on the way home. I thought of Ginger's waiting for her love with the expectant look in her wide-set eyes. I didn't chastise myself, as my daydreams were becoming a way to distract me from my growing feelings for Gerry.

While relaxing and reading my book, close to my home stop, I heard a ruckus in the front of the train car. A woman in a purple coat blocked my view of the incident. I inched my way up and saw Dr. Baldwin ministering to Eddie in what appeared to be CPR. He was barking orders to those gathering near him. I completely froze to see the star of my fantasy life, struggling for air, under the compressions of Dr. Baldwin.

With an arm waving motion, he pushed against the assembled crowd, and put his face into his hands. He mumbled the words Justin and arrhythmia, and a quietly attractive woman put a hand on his back and said, "Daniel, there's nothing more to do right now….He's gone."

Her words were echoed through the slow screeching of the braking train as it made its way to the Stanton Street stop. I would know about Eddie before Ginger knew. Before her world exploded. I knew that Ginger, whom I later learned was Amanda, would crawl through a cave of grief and maybe never return to beauty and hope. I re-lived the metallic taste of loss, and hated it.

At the Stanton Street stop, I saw Amanda with her cork-screw curls newly done, rush to the train, still oblivious to the impact of her loss, to the vicious twist her life would take.

It pained me to think of the time it would take her to notice a sunset, or laugh at a joke. To move forward through a mountain of resistance to happiness, to slivers of joy, shaky, at first, but then enduring.

I imagined for her a re-birth, perhaps in a number of years, maybe opening to a new love, different from this one, or maybe not bonded with another, but strengthened from this blow, joyful in knowing how fragile, yet precious, this life is.

From: Adelaide Magazine

THE OPENING

We were proud to be cynics, Walter and I. It made the list of things
we bantered about at parties, smug and sure-footed in our delivery.

"No taking out a loan to pay the vet in our family," Walter
would say, especially after a few cognacs. His comments often
followed my boast of never bringing the kids to Disney.

We were different, not given to maudlin fawning over animals
or their mascots.

I remember the slight shift in our dogma.

One of our landscapers, never charmed by my Spanish
pointing, " Mira señora!"

I scraped my shin in the bushes in front of Walter's office,
to see what delighted the somber guy. Draped across her young, I
saw a black feral cat. She hissed at us and we backed away.

Hector, his name sewn into his pocket, averted his eyes and
walked to his truck.

I went indoors to tell Walter, and noticed he was on his
business line. There was talk of an opening at corporate in
Naperville.

" Candace, dinner at the Drake, shopping the Miracle Mile.
You'll love it!"
Our kids were in college, and my family was in Chicago, so I let
myself warm to the idea.
When his call was finished, I grabbed his hand and led him outside
to see our visitors.

He pulled me close and said, "She's like you with Lucas that time we went to New York." Keeping a respectful distance, we lingered, enjoying the scene.

When is the last time Walter hugged me like that?, I thought, grateful for the closeness.
I often reminded myself that the luxuries we enjoyed put a strain on him, showing in the lines around his eyes.

"I wish you all good lives," he said solemnly.

In the months that followed the cats scattered. Except for one.

We learned words like tabby, shyly asking friends we may have insulted before.
We eased into feeding her, learning her preference for wet food over dry. She waited for the sound of our car the evenings we went out, looking expectant like our Ellen at two years old waiting for a treat.

When my husband broke free from work before sundown, we would relax on the back porch hoping for a visitor. Like her mother, the cat was taut and wary, never getting close. But she was close enough to bring out of us long buried memories of our kids when they were one hug away.

And we voiced present concerns as twilight slanted shadows across the lawn.

"Do you trust that guy Ellen is seeing?" Walter asked, which I left unanswered.

During one of these feline visits, we made the decision for Walter to accept the promotion.

The week before the move we recruited many of our neighbors to feed the cat. I called before showing up with a box of shredded fare, her favorite. The night before the move, Walter joined me. We hadn't bothered to befriend any of them until it was time to go.

"Be careful when you back out," Walter told a teenager on our circle.

" She doesn't go for dry food," I told another neighbor who reluctantly accepted the food I offered.

The car carrier which picked up my car screeched to a halt on our street.

That will scare her, I thought, unable to let go.

Moving day arrived. I had fixed us a cooler of goodies for the long drive. No car carrier for Walter's Audi. As we pulled out, he reached into the back seat to grab a bottle of water and I noticed his eyes scanning the circle. I couldn't, but I was grateful that our reins had been slackened.

During our first business dinner, Walter's boss made clumsy attempts to welcome us.

"Guess you'll miss the Jags?"

"We will, but my wife Candace is a Bears fan," Walter said, taking my hand.

A tiny woman with wide-set eyes and a kind face said, "What do you miss the most?"

Walter and I smiled at each other. He looked as boyish to me as he did when our coffee table was a cardboard box. I shook my head slightly trying to transmit the tuitions still to be paid, the rules of the game to be played.

"We're excited to be here. Looking forward, not back."

The tremor in our world was not yet an earthquake, but it was a start.

From: No Extra Words

HELEN SPENCER

Helen froze when she heard her name. The door of the faculty room was open.

"Of course Helen will be there. It's in her honor." Gabby's gentle voice. Helen was drawn to listen further, but tip- toed away from the area. No need to be reminded of her oddball status at Spring Hill School.

Skillful at avoiding parties, she was locked into this one. After forty years of teaching, Helen Spencer was set to retire. Piper promised to be there, and she hoped he chose to fly, his driving skills declining with age. He still took credit for getting Headmaster Martin, his old prep school buddy, to hire her. Her world expanded when referring to Piper. Although out of the house when Helen was eight, he remained a source of joy when she picked through the litter of her childhood.

The litter of bottles cracked on the floor, or hidden where she packed away her toys. Her father was able to work, not given to hangovers. His trust fund cushioned the need to excel at the bank. Her mother could sleep through the mornings, letting Helen get herself ready for school. The day Piper packed his bags for college left Helen sobbing in her room. Although part of her was happy for him, the child in her gave into her sorrow, her feelings not yet stunted by life.

It was shortly after Piper's departure when Helen started to open and close drawers, line up her toys, and lock and unlock her bedroom door. Her mother was too wasted to notice, and Helen too ashamed to speak of it. Mrs. Maxwell, her third grade teacher, spoke to her after school one day. Helen remembered the afternoon, when it was her turn to clap the chalk from the erasers, a job she could do endlessly. Mrs. Maxwell brought erasers of her own and clapped along with her in the recess yard.

"Helen," she said quietly, "I notice you like to keep your desk neat." Raised with little praise, Helen feared trouble, feared her mother's rage.

" Is that bad?" she asked. "Helen, please give this letter to your mother." Helen remembered it was one of the good spells, her mother spiffy and sober, playing the piano, inviting neighbors to bridge. From that letter grew a relationship with a doctor, who guided Helen through exercises to break her obsessive thoughts and actions. Mrs. Maxwell didn't become a villain in Mrs. Spencer's booze-fueled drama, and Helen found inspiration for her career. She chose to become a helping hand to some other child, while imparting knowledge, drawing out the riches of learning.

Before she was ready to face working, Helen armed herself with several advanced degrees and certificates. Her father, who found sobriety and a sparkling new wife, bought Helen a condo and supported her through graduate school.

Headmaster Martin didn't pepper her with questions during the initial interview, so perhaps Piper's influence was strong. She arrived at Spring Hill School prepared for the barrage of tricky tough questions she had faced in earlier interviews. One principal bombarded her with follow-up questions, which drove her to re-arrange the articles on his desk. She remembered his sneering smile when he said, " I think we're done here."

She was equipped to teach in the Upper and Lower School, but the adolescents frightened her. She settled into Spring Hill Lower School, alternating between second and third grade. From the moment she entered the classroom, her breathing slowed, her fear slackened, and she was able to concentrate on the little faces before her.

Miss Spencer didn't baby her young charges. She spoke to them directly with a patience this age group needed.

Reading was her favorite challenge, sounding out the letters with her students. Many of the little sophisticates had traveled the world and been tutored for years, so her work was lessened, but she found most children enjoyed being noticed and guided through the words before them.

When Headmaster Martin visited her classes, her focus was less gifted, but the children's natural interruptions and questions kept her from full-blown anxiety. She mentioned it to Piper during one of their chess matches, how visitation was hard for her. He may have worked his magic again, because Helen had fewer visits from her boss.

The new boss, Dr. Dan Richards was hired to replace Headmaster Martin. Helen felt frightened by the new Headmaster at first, but he proved to be a fair and even boss. Helen grew to trust him and he shared her serious nature.

Helen thanked God and her medication that she could control her OCD at school. Like a well-worn road, the crusty walls at Spring Hill threw few curves her way. Through decades of exposure to the school and her breathing and counting exercises, Miss Helen Spencer could function in the classroom with the zeal of an artist.

The children trusted and accepted her. Their sophisticated parents were often surprised when they met Miss Spencer, expecting someone hip and chic.

As Helen approached her retirement, and the dreaded public celebration, she was thankful for Gabby who arrived at Spring Hill soon after the new Headmaster. Gabby, more stylish and normal than Helen, nonetheless had a survivor's heart, having lost her husband when he was just thirty-three. Her perceptions were nearly clairvoyant, and she saw in Helen a friend.

Piper had met Helen's colleagues at Spring Hill functions, and Helen was careful to introduce him by his given name, Peter. Surviving their childhood home gave the Spencers an unbreakable bond. He arrived a few days before the celebration. Helen was so excited she set up their chess table, made reservations at Chez Pierre, and bought a bottle of scotch, aged twelve years , the way he liked it.

The day Piper arrived, Gabby insisted on driving Helen to the airport to pick him up. As they were leaving school in the June heat, several students called out to them. A little girl ran up to them..."Miss Spencer. Miss Spencer, I lost a tooth." Helen knelt down to look, the child's fist enclosed around it. Helen gently opened the little fist and regarded the tooth as a treasure.

"They will miss you, Helen, the little ones, " Gabby said with the slight lilting accent of her native Spanish.

She scheduled extra sessions with her doctor during the week before her party. He regressed her to an earlier stage, and kept his desk messy, his pen - holder laying on its side. He asked her to wear old clothing, to get her hands sticky with taffy and rub her clothing with the goo. He amped up the implosion therapy that had worked in earlier years, and he worked with her through deep-breathing exercises, her hand touching her old tee shirt with the goo.

He guided her to a formally set table where he placed a cupcake, a cleaning rag and a cup of coffee. After she was seated for three full minutes, her doctor smashed the cupcake on the table cloth, and poured some coffee into the mess.

He then asked her to continue breathing, to ignore the mess, and look up at the speaker, which was a yellow circle on the wall behind him. He reminded her he was on the board at the school, and would be on the stage to the left of the podium.

The Upper School student council decorated the auditorium for Helen's good-bye celebration. Helen's friend Gabby was in charge. The board spared no expense: fresh flowers for each table, elegant china and silverware, and finely-wrapped bags of Godiva chocolate. A popular clique of seniors stopped by and muttered something nasty about Helen, and Gabby who was crouched below a table scraping wax from the floor, shot up, walked over, and hissed "Shut up" in Spanish. Many of the students heard her and giggled. Gabby winced and hoped she didn't get fired.

Helen chose a black dress, heels, and a string of pearls. Piper turned to her and said, "You look lovely, Helen."

Shortly after the invocation, a striking young woman walked through the crowd and many of the students gasped and said, "That's Ariel!" Some of the faculty recognized her too. She was surrounded by buff men who escorted her to Dr. Richards. She leaned closely and whispered something to him. Few men would deny this newly - famous model anything.

Ariel walked up the three steps to the microphone and spoke into it.

"My name is Amber Carson."

Chants of "Ariel" began to emerge from the crowd. Dr. Richards in his deepest growl said "Let her speak!" The students obeyed.

Ariel continued in a clear, confident voice. "I was a student at Spring Hill. and I came here to honor Miss Spencer, my second grade teacher. I was gawky, I stuttered, and I was often taunted by the other kids. I remember the day Miss Spencer sat with me on the old stone wall next to the playground. And changed my life."

Helen remembered the sessions she had with Amber. Miss Spencer was careful to spread school books on the desk between them to look like a normal tutoring session. Helen taught Amber breathing and counting exercises to do before she spoke. She promised Amber that she would only call on her when she raised her hand, when she was ready to speak. Helen also made Amber walk erectly with a book on her head to honor her natural height, to square her shoulders, to ground her steps, to fake confidence in herself.

Many in the audience stood and snapped photos of Ariel, cell phones bobbing all through the room. Ariel hesitated, and Helen was thrust back in time to young Amber, recognizing the frightened pained look of struggle.

Helen walked elegantly to the stage ,whispered to Ariel, and they nodded to the audience,

Helen grabbed the mic confidently, and Ariel took a seat with the board.

Miss Spencer felt no fear as she spoke into the mic, the fruits of her vocation thrusting her to take action to soothe a student, albeit a famous, successful student, the model Ariel. Helen was gracious and elegant in her words to all assembled and gave thanks to her mentor, the late Mrs. Maxwell, who through the dusty chalk gave her a glimmer of hope.

Hope that let Helen carve through a mountain of mental anguish to touch the little souls of Spring Hill School.

From: Potluck Magazine

DANCING IN WINTER

Later in the evening, I remembered how I knew the soft-spoken
woman near the patio. Laura convinced me to join her at the
Sidwells' summer party. The bartender splashed the bar with
frosty mojitos garnished with mint sprigs and lime. Laura floated
throughout the crowd, while I took refuge in a corner seat near
Karen Resnick. I didn't know who knew details about me or about
how I spent the month of January. My refuge,
Karen, seemed transfixed by a rotating sprinkler outside.

The party crowd had emigrated from the Northeast to Florida.
The hosts skillfully separated Yankee fans from the Red Sox
crowd. Michael and I weren't big sports fans, but I reminded
myself, once again, that Michael's interests had changed.

When Michael accepted a position in the economics
department at Palm Beach County University, we were both
excited about the move. "Katie, can you picture us swimming
outside in winter?" he said while Sophie was trying out cartwheels
between us in our toy-cluttered living room. Joyfully, we decided
to move to Florida.

Laura interrupted my reverie in the corner seat. " Katie, let's
bail!" Her mood began to improve as soon as we cleared the
Sidwell property. " The party was a dud, but at least you went,
Katie" she said as she nearly skipped to her silver Nissan.

I had met Laura at one of Michael's boring faculty parties, and
she and I had clicked, bonded, insert any cliché for platonic love at

first sight. She'd been in and out of a short marriage and was finishing her PhD at Palm County U. Although I was eager to return home to Sophie, Laura was my driver, and she pulled into the Blue Moon Lounge without checking with me. A suburban summer party was one thing: entering a pick-up joint was another.

Luckily, there were few people at the bar. The bar itself was a rusty granite that reminded me of the kitchen in our old home up north. The bartender looked
to be the age of your average prom date. Laura, who never missed an opportunity to charm, straightened up and asked the bartender his name. She then asked Chris for two chardonnays, and I interjected that I would have a Pelligrino with ice and lime. "You know I can't drink with my meds, " I hissed under my breath. Our rapport had the intense sister-like closeness that allowed for endless hisses, corrections and nudgings. "Oh Katie, we're celebrating! One glass of wine is not going to have you keel over on the floor." " So m'am, what will it be?"

"Oh no," I thought . " That m'am thing." "Do I look my age or is it simply southern manners. I sipped my sparkling water, worrying that Sophie might not like her babysitter, but kept myself from sending texts. Sophie was smart enough to grab the sitter's cell if things were too uncomfortable.

We moved to Florida in the summer so Sophie could start school with her third grade class. Michael had found our Florida home close to the university. It took me a while to adjust to the pastels in our neighborhood - so many houses painted like Easter eggs, so unlike "up north," as everybody called the entire Northeast.

Our new home was in walking distance from the beach, and the three of us rarely missed an evening strolling along the water's edge. Should I have savored those precious moments more, or would they have been tinged with horror and terror had I known what was coming?

Laura dropped me off to a very relieved Sophie. It's not that she didn't like the babysitter, whose name I had trouble remembering. It's more that these days, Sophie can't hide her need for me under her rolled eyes and shoulder shrugs. After I whispered good night to her, as she pulled her knees to her chest, I remembered the name of the woman on the Sidwell's patio - Elena.

"You look good, Katie. Don't be nervous about meeting my colleagues, " Michael said while squeezing my knee. We were en route to the party where I met Laura. She steered me on to a window seat and revealed herself to me from the moment I sat down. She had a wide-eyed, almost vacant look, as she paid close attention to my responses , drawing me out and relaxing me amidst Michael's colleagues.

I noticed Michael giving his attention to a man and woman nearly as tall as he. Although never in the military, Michael presented himself with the command presence of a soldier. Michael laughed aloud, and I was relieved that he, too, was enjoying himself. Earlier, he had steered me away from a German prof and his severe - looking wife, warning me that they were pretentious and boring. Many of the profs were stiff and self-important, making me doubly glad Laura had reached out to me.

" Who were those tall people you were talking to? " I asked Michael on our way home. "They're in my department, " he said in a neutral tone. I tried to ignore the tightening in my chest. The absence of detail struck me as weird. I thought about Sophie and how this move might affect her. She feigned sleep when we arrived home from the party.

During our walk along the water's edge the first day of winter, Sophie's cartwheels matched the scurrying of the sand pipers. "Daddy, you're not paying attention!" she wailed with the vehemence of the confident only child. I didn't need Sophie to draw my attention to the remote chilliness of her dad's mood. Michael tickled her and she squealed with delight, and her brown eyes locked on me lovingly. Confident of her dad's affection, she didn't try to short me in any way. She never did.

I whispered to Michael that Sophie would surely sleep well and squeezed his hand trying to stoke the spark between us. I also decided to buy a dazzling new dress for New Year's Eve. The hinting didn't create the closeness I had hoped for, as Michael worked in his office, even after Sophie had fallen asleep.

After my family was gone the next day, I drove to the mall surrounded by palm trees and lush with blooming hibiscus plants and bougainvillea. I found the dress I had imagined within the first hour. I loved the way it clung to me and cinched my waist, but I needed another's opinion. The sales woman assured me that the dress was flattering and stylish, and I made a decision to model it for Michael.

No rustic bridges or ivy lined walls surround Palm County U. It shines with the pastels of our neighborhood, complete with hurricane-proof glass and sturdy new buildings. After finding an area to change into my new dress, I approached Michael's office. His secretary, a retired school teacher with a silver helmet of hair, stood up and thrust her arm forward like a crossing guard. " Dr. Mike can not see you right now. He's working with a student on his dissertation". Her hesitant speech and darting eyes belied her words.

That evening, I grilled Michael about his day, whom he saw, what he was working on. My intensity shone through or his secretary spoke of my visit. " You know, Katie."
"Know what?" I stammered, spilling coffee on my favorite blue blouse. "That there's someone else. I have never felt this way." "it's Tara, isn't it!" I screamed referring to the long-legged woman from the faculty party. I had since learned she was his assistant in the business school. " No" I whispered trying to shield myself from the truth that he had spoken, the probable rupture of our marriage. " Maybe if we hadn't moved here, " I said desperately, as he rinsed his coffee cup and looked at me, his brown eyes so like our daughter's. "But Michael....Sophie's first steps...You were there!" I wailed as I threw my cup into the sink, bent over as if struck by a baseball bat.

During the week that followed, I was unable to sleep and became disorganized, disheveled and morose. I knew that Sophie needed me as strongly as she had as an infant. But I lost control. I began drinking heavily, catching only fragments of sleep, pacing around the house. I cried uncontrollably, squelching the sounds so Sophie wouldn't hear me.

I have vague memories of Laura and Michael strapping me into the car and windshield wipers flapping with a rapid swooshing sound. I remember bright lights, blankets and a nurse with a large needle. Questions, endless questions, from strangers treading softly around me.

The medicine lulled me into the blackened quiet of sleep. " Katie, you are in a hospital," Aubrey Brant, M.D., said to me. His name tag hung loosely from his white coat. " Do you wish to hurt yourself or anyone else?" He asked me with a dignified British accent. My eyes drooped, and my mouth felt like cotton candy as I nodded   "no. " At no time, before or since, had I lied so completely. " Where's Sophie?" I croaked. " With her father," Dr. Brant assured me.

Moments later, a nurse dressed in a drab orange smock escorted me to my first inpatient group meeting. En route, I wondered if she had chosen that color to remind us we were in jail. Although my senses were numbed with meds, I knew the best way to return to Sophie was to cooperate with the program.

Each of us was encouraged to share our story - our pain with the group. I couldn't, wouldn't. "Michael should be here, not me! " I wanted to shout to the group:" Michael betrayed me!"

I didn't feel crazy, but knew I must have been to lose control of my role as mother. One evening, the nurse in the orange smock caught me throwing out the meds that were delivered to me; my name hugging a little plastic cup, as if that cup could define or defend me.

During Michael's first visit he delivered the death knell to our marriage, coloring the blows with words - young, alive, happy. I refused to ask him about Tara : gave him no opening to expand on his newfound joy.

He brought Sophie with him for a short visit during my second week, and we hugged each other fiercely. Seeing her strengthened my resolve to heal and become strong.

Dr. Brant listened to me. He did not gush or smile at me, but he did listen, his English accent jarring me at times to the present- to the endless pain in my soul. He introduced me to Elena one sunny morning in January. Her specialty was dance therapy. She exuded warmth and compassion. Her devotion to her art flowed through her every move, her lilting voice encouraging us to flow along with her. Most of my classmates moved as stiffly as I. Few smiled. But as the days turned into weeks, the promise of bright skies and laughter, whispering to us through the lyrics of her music, fortified us to heal, to want to sing again.

Group therapy sessions continued. I began to find them comforting and to develop a relationship with the other patients, ranging from police officers to single mothers.

While listening to Dr. Brant's melodious voice, I felt movement return to my stiff limbs. Coupled with Elena's dance classes, and our daily walks outside in the January sun, I was beginning to breathe more deeply, and to catch myself giggling and smiling again.

After screaming at Michael the day before my discharge, I called Laura and asked if she would escort me home. She did. I clung to Sophie in the foyer, noticing that my wedding photo no longer stood on the wobbly wooden table on the right. Grabbing on to what poise and dignity I had, with my cotton mouth, glazed eyes and hesitant gait, I walked into my kitchen and stared coolly at my husband, Michael. Although he owned a key to another residence, he looked comfortable leaning against the bar. He matched my stare with a steely cold look. How had this happened to us? His look told me that he would not reverse his decision.

He remained at home with me in our guest bedroom, moving out only after I became less wobbly, and better able to care for Sophie, and the details of home management. He refused to accept couples' counseling from Dr. Brant or anyone else.

Throughout the spring, I met with Sophie's teachers, attended her sporting events, and tried to ignore the hollow sounds of our home without her father. I insisted Sophie direct her questions about our new life to her dad, trying desperately to shield her from the depth of my grief.

By the time Laura invited me to join her at the Sidwell's party, I felt slightly less bereft and abandoned, more like the Katie whom I knew, more like myself. I decided I would pay a visit to Elena at the hospital to thank her for her loving work with me and my fellow patients. As I approached her office, I caught a look at myself in the mirror and saw joy in my reflection. It reminded me of Sophie's joy when she took her first steps. Nimble - footed, I advanced to Elena's office.

" Katie, it's so good to see you." At that moment Dr. Brant walked by, and she beckoned him in. They both treated me warmly. Elena mentioned that I didn't seem to recognize her at the party. " Delayed reaction. There's a lot of that these days." "I was very surprised to see you with Miss Laura," Elena said fervently.

All the color drained from Dr. Brant's face. He asked me to follow him to his office. As I sat in the familiar chair, looking out onto the grounds of the hospital, my mind raced with possibilities. "Had Sophie been in an accident? But how would he know that? "

" Katie, Michael and I made the decision to withhold some pertinent information from you. We thought it better for you to carry on that way," his nervousness apparent, his English accent more pronounced. " Michael's love interest attended the party with you this weekend."

I clasped my hand over my mouth, gagging and trying not to scream. "Please tell me you're lying, Dr. Brant!" " I wish I were," he said gently. " Dear Katie, I wish I were."

I felt a suffocating suction in my chest. " Are you telling me it's not Tara?" I whispered to Dr. Brant, who had come around his desk and squeezed my shoulders from behind. "It's Laura, my close friend Laura?" " Yes Katie" he whispered quietly.

The late afternoon shadows slanted across the doctor's office. Dr. Brant sat quietly, while I tried to absorb this blow. My numbed senses felt like the early days of Elena's dance. The taste of betrayal fueled my rage, but whetted my desire to survive. I thought of Sophie's first smile, her first steps. Scorching anger pulsed through me as I made my way out of the hospital to my car. A beam of sunlight blinded my vision, but not my resolve to dance again, to swirl and bend like the palm trees around me, to stretch and grow with my brown-eyed daughter.

From: Potluck Magazine

BEHIND THE TREES

Max held Daddy's little shovel, digging in the dirt.

"That's Daddy's shovel, Max."

"Lexie, it's a trowel, and Daddy won't mind."

I knew Max was right about Daddy. Saturday morning he caught us eating chocolate ice cream for breakfast, and he just patted Max's head, when he took Harry for his walk.
And when Miss Dixon called Daddy into school cause Max wasn't doing his homework, Max was still allowed to ride his bike and play basketball.

"You should wear Mommy's gardening gloves," I said as he poured the seeds into rows he had dug. He handed me Mommy's sprinkling can and asked me to pour a little water on the rows.

"Why aren't you planting them in the usual place?" I asked.

"Cause I want it to be a surprise," he said, gently rolling his hand over the dirt.

Ruby caught us behind the trees Kentucky Derby Day. Daddy was at a party up the street. Ruby was stricter than Daddy, and didn't want us that far from the house.

She got tears in her eyes when she saw the rows of yellow on their little stems.

"Y'all need to come back near the yard where I can see you."

On Flag Day, it took both Daddy and Ruby to wheel Mommy out to see the flowers my brother had planted. Max didn't even bother to change out of his Safety Patrol belt, he was so excited. When he got the belt muddy, Daddy didn't say anything bad

Daddy didn't say anything at all.

From: Rain, Party & Disaster Society

THE FLOWER SHOP

Angie and I loved making deliveries. She drove the truck well, and I didn't, so we made a good team. We had worked at Keller's Flower Shop since high school, and were closing in on college graduation, so the place didn't bug us as it sometimes did when there was no exit in sight.

Mimi Keller inherited the shop from her parents, and she added the pizzazz and charm the place needed. Her nimble fingers picked through flowers with an artist's eye. Her baskets and vases meshed color and form into masterpieces. The shop was busy.

The owner hired Angie and me as a package deal. Newly sixteen, we arrived at job interviews together, brazenly insisting they needed us both. When we met Mimi she hired us both right away. She had twin daughters, so maybe she didn't find dealing in twos unusual.

Rachel and Jody had been urging their mom to let them work at Keller's since we started. Mimi put the twins on clean- up duty, a job that was losing its luster as they entered high school. We didn't know their dad too well, but there was no mistaking they were his. Their thick auburn hair and aquiline features bore little resemblance to Mimi.

" It's as if I weren't even there," Mimi would say, "they look so much like John Randall." She was clearly in love with her husband, and often used his full name. Angie and I knew she was also proud of keeping her own name. She was a Keller, and everybody in town knew her as such.

Most people knew we worked at Keller's and called out " Angie! Chrissy!" when they saw the truck go by.

"Chrissy, there is nothing wrong with being a townie," Angie often reminded me.

"Yeah, but the boarders think we're scum." I would tell her.

"None of those pampered creeps could ever work like we do."

The pampered creeps were our classmates at Chester College, which was in walking distance from the Flower Shop. Angie felt no shame driving the truck through the streets of the college. I ducked down in the seat when we passed the campus Starbucks, until Angie mocked me out of it. It was the week before Valentine's Day. We were surrounded by roses, exquisite and fragrant. Angie yelled out to the crowd at Starbucks, and my slouching days were over.

Not only was Mimi Keller a fair boss, Angie and I liked her, and shared her love of flowers. She would ask our opinion while pulling together an arrangement, her pink rubber gloves in the air. We told her the truth, that the white lilies needed something colorful, like African violets, or the lavender orchid was wimpy. She respected us and eventually trusted us with a key to the shop.

"I'm going to be prepared this Mother's Day," Mimi told us pursing her lips as she did when determined. "You girls may have to let yourselves in around then. If I miss the twins' recital another year, there will be no living with them."

Angie and I exchanged a look, finding the twins hard on their mom. We noticed their Michael Kors bags and hair styled at Sensations, the cost of such things beyond us. Angie's Uncle Tony sometimes hooked her up, no kids of his own to spoil. And Angie often split the spoils with me, like the time she gave me her gift card to Sensations for my cousin's wedding.

"They mark John Randall on a curve," Mimi continued. "I guess it's how kids are with their dads. John can do no wrong."

That very day we saw John Randall, as we thought of him, going into the bank, his charcoal suit adding to his dignified carriage. The shock of auburn hair was so like his daughters. He was truly handsome. I could see how Mimi was wacky over him.

I mentioned this to Angie and she said, "I think he's too stiff. Not my type."

"You don't get a vote on Mimi's taste." I told her as we were gearing up for the Easter rush.

" We've got to let Mimi know Easter is exam week," Angie said as we approached a two story colonial with a vase filled with orange and yellow tulips, so spring - like, so special. Mimi screened the recipients of our labor, the town's being so known. She didn't risk our safety when her full-time guys could venture into parts unknown.

" Chrissy, please warn Mimi. You have a way with her. Tell her if we keep busting our butts for her, we won't graduate."

" Yeah, I'll wait for her husband and the twin brats to be there when I say that."

" Listen to you, talking trash, like that," she said, and I felt chastened and guilty for trying to be cool. More seriously, Angie grabbed my sleeve and made me look at her.

" Chrissy, You're good. Don't lose that," she said, and I had to look away.

When we returned to Keller's, we inhaled the scents of gardenias and lilies of the valley.
Mimi gestured to the bundles and said, " A fresh shipment. Heavenly, aren't they?" None of us tired of the magic of flowers.

While adding a bow to a baby girl arrangement, Mimi asked, "Could you two clip the ends of the lilies before storing them?"

Angie handed me the cutting shears and blurted, " Mimi, Easter week is a problem." I rolled my eyes, like she took my job of telling. I had been rehearsing my lines in the truck as we skidded across a few icy patches.

Angie explained how busy we'd be with school, and Mimi told us her husband could help out. "He does the books, collects the sales, and makes bank deposits, so he knows the shop... and the neighborhood."

"I don't want to think about losing you two when you graduate," Mimi said affectionately.

I felt myself tear up, and I think Angie did too, though she'd never admit it.

Bringing a burst of cold air with him, John Randall brushed by us and pulled Mimi aside. She smiled at him, hugged him, and they spoke quietly. He'd never taken the time to get to know us, but Angie and I didn't expect him to.

Cutting shears resting in my hand, I let myself picture being with a John Randall of my own. I realized I was staring at Mimi's husband, and continued to trim the lilies laid out before me. Keller's cutting table needed a replacement. Too many nights left me fighting with a splinter from my work.

We survived the exams with lots of late nights at the campus library or Angie's house. Her family was so proud of her scholastic life, her mother set up a work/study area in the den. Her Uncle Tony stuck his head in to cheer her on, including me in his pep talks.

" You kids are doing us proud," his face often smudged with soot from the fires he fought.

When we were too shot to sit up, we sprawled on Angie's bed, our lap tops and books spread about us. We didn't do this too often, as Angie respected her mother's feelings about the study den.

We were in the den on a crisp spring day, our graduation invitations stacked on the table before us. "Is it pushy to invite people, like we're looking for presents?" I asked Angie.

"Leave it to you, Chrissy, to worry what people think," she said, as she looked up at me, her pen in hand. "I'm about to address Mimi's. Should I just put the Randall family?"

"I think Rachel and Jody would like to see their names on it. Kids don't get much snail mail," I said, careful not to talk trash about them again. Angie was a tougher boss than Mimi.

"Too many names. I'm putting the Randall family. Do you think they will come?"

I told her I couldn't imagine Mimi's missing it, and the twins might be singing at the ceremony.

When we arrived at Keller's after school the next day, Mimi was in a great mood.

"The twins' recital will be a week before Mother's Day, so this place won't be such a madhouse. I may just ask you to pick up a few deliveries the night I'm busy."

We took pride in our work, but we were relieved that Mimi would be with us for the Mother's Day crazies.

The evening of the recital, I arrived at the shop before Angie. I decided to let myself in and place the flowers in the truck. The flower shop was as quiet as a church at dawn. I took a few steps and bumped into the cutting table. It was then that I saw John Randall looking tenderly down at Mark Collins. His right hand cupped Mark's jaw, and his left clutched the buttons of Professor Collins's jacket. I couldn't breathe. I almost screamed.

Stricken. The word that entered my jumbled brain. Mimi's husband looked stricken when he saw me. Mark had moved to another part of the shop, leaving John and me together.

"Deliveries," I managed to say.

"My job tonight," he said.

I made my way to my car, grateful that Angie was late.

I trusted her, but needed time to absorb the shock of what I'd seen. I thought of Mimi and started to cry. And yet, I had never seen her husband look so comfortable, so at home with himself. I was horrified and moved by the loving embrace I stumbled upon.

Angie's car pulled up, and I had visions of one of Uncle Tony's pool hall buddies making little of John Randall. I tried to pull myself together to keep this to myself.

Angie knew me too well.

I hugged her fiercely, and said, "Your car. Your room."

"I'll kill him." she growled, when I could bring myself to talk.

Never being a fan of his, Angie continued in this mode till she caught the look on my face. "What is wrong with you, Chrissy?" her loyalty to Mimi as big as her heart.

I was too stunned to say much.

"He looked happy, Angie."

"Don't you care about Mimi?" she said.

This pierced me in a way that only Angie could. Like wind whipping up before a storm, Angie's mood changed. She saw she had hurt me, and was beginning to accept what I saw.

"I'll bet she knows," Angie said. I let this sink in, knowing I would never reveal it to Mimi. In the way shock lets normal thoughts through, I realized we had never been so quiet in Angie's room.

"Why do you think she knows, Ang?"

"Simple. Because she loves him."

Dreading my next shift at work, I practiced looking normal in the mirror. I applied my make-up with care, hoping Mimi didn't see any change in me. Mimi pulled me into her office as soon as I arrived. She looked haggard. She knew...... but I was sure.... she was just as shocked as I. "John told me." Three words with the power to explode her universe.

" It's new to me...... We're talking....He does love me, Chrissy, " she whispered.

Straightening her shoulders she switched gears, realizing she had said too much.

" John and I accept the invitation to your graduation," she said with a weak smile.

"Angie and I would be honored," was all I could manage to say. I grabbed her hand with both of mine and said. "Only Angie have I told. Nobody else, I promise."

After a few awkward days at work, Mimi and I had an unspoken understanding. If I said I hadn't told Angie, she would have seen the lie, and there would be little between us. As the days grew into weeks, we accepted each other as two women who knew the other well. And she trusted I said nothing to others.

There was also among the three us, Angie, Mimi and me, the melancholy of an ending, and the memories of our time together at Keller's Flower Shop.

Graduation day was spectacular. Chester College Commencement was outdoors on a sunny June evening. Angie picked me up in the new Jeep Uncle Tony had given her. We arrived amidst a sea of flowers surrounding the stage. They were hauntingly familiar, all those flowers.

We stood together on the stage looking out at the guests, and I saw Mimi and John.

They were smiling at the twins, who were to our right in gold choir gowns. The sun was setting behind them, and I saw the blend of color, vibrant, complex, yet simple in its beauty, much like love itself.

From: The Furious Gazelle

MULTI-COLORED RIBBONS

Tammy slammed the lid on the spaghetti pot.

"Shh," I said. "Calvin doesn't want a bad report."

"Don't worry about him. He's kind of sweet on ya," she said, with traces of the Georgia Peach she might have been.

We weren't used to the industrial - sized kitchen utensils.

Our last job was at a half-way house with an incongruous, but lovely purple orchid hanging from the porch. It had a regular kitchen with normal-sized pots and pans.

There's no pretty way to put it. Tammy and I met in the slammer. I remember my eyelids stuck together and trace memories of being dragged along a cold, dark, corridor. As I pushed open my eyes, more ugly pictures flashed through my mind....breaking the glass in the hospital pharmacy, stealing the oxy and whatever else I could grab, landing with a thud on a bench.

Tammy and I clicked from the start. Her sins were much like mine...an addict who flew out of control. Her hair was speckled with sunlit hues, and her southern accent was still with her in Philly.

When we completed our time, we were assigned to Calvin Johnson, a probation officer who hated his job, and wasn't too keen on the people he managed.

Calvin reluctantly escorted us into his office, made less shabby by a picture of his son's full grin. When Tammy said "Yes sir," "No sir," he shot me a look like, "Is this one for real?" And I said, "Mr. Johnson, Tammy grew up in Atlanta."

Settled. Done. Philly speak for so many things...

Calvin had just finished an in-service training about matching community service to the skills of the offender. He actually read from a sheet, with a similar tone of an officer reading our Miranda rights.

Mid way through his recitation, he let out a sigh and said, "Other than being loser druggies, anything you're good at?"

We took it from there, interrupting one another with our desire to cook, cater, prepare and serve food. Our kitchen duties inside were our favorite.

When I was still able to care for Ashley, I used to love to try out new recipes on her, mashed into the only bowl she liked. In spite of the data against sugar, I often added a teaspoon to whatever I made, just so my food taster would eat it.

She squealed with delight when I pulled out my cupcake tray, knowing she would taste the sugar that she craved.

When Tammy and I were in jail, I tortured myself with thoughts of the sugar I shouldn't have given my daughter...feared I was fueling the addictions I may have passed on to her.

""Honey, Tammy would say as we raked the jail's garden. Kids like sugar. You didn't invent that." When I no longer could keep my whirling thoughts to myself, Tammy would get the full unadulterated vent.

"Susan," she would say, reaching her muddy hand around my back. "You're going to get her back. "

If I live to be a hundred years old, I will never forget her kindness to me.

Calvin, as we came to call him, seemed pleased with our zeal, and his hesitation about Tammy's other ness eased into a hint of a smile.

Which brought us to our community service in the half-way house. We were to arrive no later than seven A.M. to prepare a plethora of choices, as many of our residents were fueling for jobs they were hoping to keep.

Tammy and I settled in easily to the work. We agreed we wouldn't try to befriend the residents, but to concentrate on our work, and getting through our probation.

On the morning I had perfected my pancakes, I heard a baritone behind me.

"Susan, you missed your labs this week."

"Cal....Mr. Johnson, I wasn't expecting you," I said, baffled that I'd missed the appointment. How much had addiction stolen from me?

Wary of the stranger, one of the guys at the pancake table stood up and reached a wiry arm to shake Calvin's hand. "Susan here, is busy feeding us, sir."

I blinked back tears at the man's loyalty to me. I think he knew Calvin was a government worker, complete with the beige sedan parked out front.

I burned my hand on the griddle in my haste to speak to Calvin privately.

With a slight head tilt, I directed him to the living area.

"You may not believe me, but I'm not using. I was so nervous about this placement, I forgot about my lab tests," I said, while looking directly at him.

He leaned back slightly against the overstuffed chair behind him.

"Susan," he said, "This is no way to get your child back."

I was surprised how much it mattered that he thought less of me.

"Calvin, I'm trying to get it right!   The probation, the community service...I lost sight of my Wednesday labs. My place is cluttered with cookbooks hoping to make the grade here...hoping to get an A in community service."

"That's all well and good....but you gotta prove you're clean...every...single....day... if need be."

Tammy, sensing I needed her, left the guys in the kitchen to join us.

"This isn't your concern," he said to Tammy.

I winced slightly at his tone, but remembered my goal, my child.

Visions of the social worker and all the forms I signed, still shaking in the detox unit pushed Tammy right out of my head. If

Calvin had a pick on her, it was nothing compared to my quest to reunite with Ashley.

In our initial meeting with Calvin, I imagined community service where I could see my daughter. A week after he chose our site, I asked if I could see a list of our choices, as he determined our first rotation would be three weeks.

The Wilson Community Center nearly popped off the page. Kevin, one of our fellow inmates, a cop who had lost much...even his pension, still had contacts everywhere.

I remember how I clutched myself, as if shot, when he found the foster family who cared for Ashley. It was on the same street as Wilson, a city facility newly completed that shone amid the old Philly dwellings.

I asked Calvin if he could place us there next, and he patiently explained we needed to complete our rotation in the half-way house. I wasn't devastated by this news, as I needed time to adjust for rehearsing what I would say to Ash, and how I would say it.

She was nearly six years old, and she had been with the same family since my arrest. Kevin's sources were on target in all fields of civil service and civil law. Ashley was enjoying twin sisters, a little older than she, in her placement family. The Mitchell's twins were their biological children, and Ashley was reportedly happy there.

Kevin, our ex-cop inmate, was tuned into my reaction to this news , mixed at best, jealous to the quick of this family, when Tammy and I saw him at NA meetings. Sometimes, I had to stop myself from grilling him with questions, instead of asking how he was doing, trusting that he wasn't using.

When I could no longer stand it, I asked Kevin what was Mrs. Mitchell's first name.

"Susan, I really can't keep revealing stuff to you. My life is enough of a mess without some new charges about privacy law," and as he stubbed out his cigarette, he said, "Janet. Janet and Rob Mitchell."

"Stay well, ladies," he said, his nickname for us, as he headed out the door of the church where we went to meetings.

"She would have a name like Janet," I hissed to Tammy. "She's probably in the PTA and the 4H club, if there's still such a thing."

"So darling," she said with an exaggerated drawl, " You want Miss Mitchell to be a junkie?'

I came to a halt and gave her a look and she said, "Sorry, Susan...that was low."

"I'm sorry, too. It's just since my parents died, I don't have anybody to vent with.
They tell us not to look for excuses, but I think losing them got me started on the stuff."

"And with your cushy life, you sure weren't prepped for jail and diner work," she said with that lop-sided smile I'd come to love.

"Let's catch this bus," she said, taking off into a sprint to the corner.

Tammy and I enjoyed our time in the half-way house, and some of the residents appeared healthier; less ashen and disappointed. We settled into the morning shift in time to hit the diner we worked in by late afternoon. The owner knew me and barely asked us to fill out paper work to be servers where the strongest drink was coffee.

When I wasn't working, I became a regular at Wilson Community Center and was delighted to see so many children playing there. If the Mitchell family lived right up the street, there was no reason my Ashley wouldn't be among the happy children swinging and sliding, uninhibited with joy.

And then I saw her, skipping between two beautiful little girls, each of whom had multi-colored ribbons in their hair, as did Ash. The self-absorbed addict in me resented those ribbons, coiled me into a stoop, as I peeked at the woman behind them smiling broadly.

There was a convenient, tattered green sign stating the rules, the kinds of rules I wished I'd lived, so I wouldn't be crouching and fearful in the presence of my own child. The foursome went by with the twins bantering that Ashley was a better sister than the other twin. It was playful and twin-like, and Ashley giggled and cast them each a look of pure love.

Janet Mitchell didn't know me yet, as I had been procrastinating filling out the forms for supervised visitation. Still wobbly from rehab, I didn't want to tarnish Ashley's life any more than I had. Calvin promised to help me, and I knew he would.....when I was ready. And the evening of the Ashley sighting, before our NA meeting, Kevin told me the Mitchell family was considering filing for adoption of my child. Breaking his vow of silence, he steered me outside to the smoking section, his eyes darting wildly. I feared he was using again.

" Susan, my sources tell me that family wants to adopt your kid."

The next thing I remember was his cradling my arm with one of his own.

"Susan, I thought we were losing you," he said.

Knowing his sources were infallible, I reached into a part of myself that had lain dormant for too long. I was going to get my child back. I started by asking Kevin to get the word out that I wanted a meeting with Janet and Rob Mitchell. Screw the red tape. If they had fallen in love with Ashley, they would break a rule or two.

But Tammy and I, now committed to a rotation at Wilson Community Center, were preparing spaghetti for a high school football team, when she slammed the lid on the pot and I shushed her about Calvin. We'd had to adjust our diner schedule to fit in some evenings at Wilson.

To say that my first meeting with Janet Mitchell was memorable, doesn't quite capture it. After initial awkwardness and fearfulness, and many drawn out silences, there wasn't the adversarial hostility I expected. Maybe I can thank Ashley who had spotted me at Wilson on a class trip, and broke from the crowd with a "Mommy" that could be heard in Tammy's Atlanta.

I held my daughter, letting the tears flow freely, and told her I was coming to her new house soon. That Mommy had done some stupid things, but was trying to get better.

The children were out with Bob Mitchell the day I met Janet. When we began to relax, we clicked. We liked each other beyond our joint caring for Ashley, as we began to traverse the delicate minefield of Ashley's future. Her husband let Janet decide what she thought best for Ashley, and I was willing to allow for ample visitation rights, if they withdrew their quest for adoption. And they did.

Both Calvin and Kevin used their tentacles to get me legal help to plead my case to the courts to re-gain custody of my child.

Ashley didn't lose her other family, although her sisters became more like cousins, as she spent much of her time in my care.

In the way that our children's lives pass by quickly, I found myself shopping with Ash for school supplies for high school. I understood and enjoyed how taken the Mitchell twins were with our unusual living arrangement; Uncle Calvin, who now sold cars; Uncle Kevin who had become a master mechanic; Aunt Tammy who cut their hair, and added the slash of purple to Ashley's that they thought was so cool.

There are times when I shudder in the middle of the night, when I think of how close I came to losing my child, but I console myself that had I relapsed, she would have been surrounded by good people who loved her.....and few of us can ask for more than that.

From: Scarlet Leaf Review

PEEKING THROUGH THE CURTAINS

Jack didn't share my interest in our new neighbors. He had chosen
our house without my seeing it. There simply wasn't time. His
transfer came up so quickly, and I needed to give notice to the
hospital before the move.

From the day we pulled into the short driveway, I had an
eerie feeling about the place. Jack was able to read me so well, I
avoided eye contact during our first tour of 19 Turner Rd.

The rooms were small, and the place felt choppy. He said,
"Kim,
I know you prefer open space and a great room, but in this
neighborhood, that's hard to find."

I pulled him to me and said, "Jack, It's fine. I'd be happy with
you on Saturn or Mars."

In his haste to find something, he accepted a year's lease in
a furnished home. My first day alone, I sat in each of the overstuffed living and dining room chairs, feeling a little like
Goldilocks. I meant what I said to Jack about my happiness, but
the house was really creeping me out. And I felt myself drawn to
checking out our neighbors.

During one of my early trips to the supermarket, I met Charles
and Anna, or more accurately, I met Charles, and studied Anna,
her pale drawn face and flat eyes. Boisterous in his greeting,
Charles introduced himself and his wife, and repeated Jack and my

names in his welcome. Anna neither smiled nor spoke. He cradled her elbow as he led her to the car, and opened her car door. The courtly gesture both touched and rattled me.

As Jack and I lingered over our chicken marsala, I brought up my meeting the neighbors. Clinking his wine glass to mine, he said, "So Charles opens the door for his wife, and this is a problem?" he said, his full wattage smile letting me know how silly I sounded.

"I know they're older and all....but she seems like, I don't know......a shell or something," trailing off, knowing Jack was under scrutiny from his supervisors, and needed to unwind and relax.

Shifting gears, I took his hand and asked him about his day.

The next day, I watched Anna walk slowly through her side yard, her face devoid of any expression. Her husband didn't appear to be home, and I nearly walked out back to strike up a conversation with her, but chickened out, determined to mind my own business.

Knowing that my interest was growing into an obsession, I chastised myself one rainy afternoon, when the buzzer from my oven startled me from my perch at the window. I wanted to know what was up next door.

Having no time to make friends, I went to my desk and retrieved the yellow paper from the waste basket. Written in neat block letters, an invitation to a Potluck Dinner a few doors down from us. While not my thing, and less so Jack's, I felt it may be a way to get to know Charles and Anna Butler.

Before I could change my mind, I called the number to accept and offer to bring lasagna.

Katie Dowling answered during the second ring.

When I introduced myself, her warmth seemed to flow through the phone.

"Kim, we'll be so happy to see you and your husband. We didn't want to barge in, and ...we planned it, hoping you'd come. I was going to drop by tomorrow to invite you.

Don't worry about bringing anything...just yourselves. Do you two drink wine and beer?"

"Yes. Thank you, Katie," I said, relieved by her welcome.

As soon as I hung up I called my sister Carolyn to tell her about it. First, I apologized for being a phone stalker, as I'd been bugging her since a week before the move.

"Good for you, Kim. And when you find a job, you'll meet lots of people."

I told her I thought the woman next door was under some kind of a spell or something.

"Kim," she said, in her older sister voice, "I hope you're not blowing this up in your head. Has the move been hard on you?"

"No. Carolyn, I'm fine. I just don't want to bother Jack right now. I can see his mind whirling with his new job, and he doesn't need me dragging him down," I said.

I asked about her husband and kids and when I hung up, I felt that... all is right with the world feeling my sister gave me.

Later that evening, Jack surprised me with flowers, wine, and an upbeat reaction to the gathering. "Sounds good," he said, as I was placing the soft yellow roses on the dining room table.

As it turned out, Jack was unable to free himself from a working dinner, so I ventured to the Dowling's party alone. Clutching a chilled bottle of chardonnay, I tapped on their door, and heard a chorus of "Come in!"

Multi-colored balloons surrounded the couch and dining room table.

The Dowling children darted from room to room, jumping up to show me the balloons,

"Careful, you guys," Katie said, through a big smile.

Each balloon said "Welcome," and Katie guided me to see the cake her kids were clearly ready to eat. It said, "Welcome Kim and Jack."

I blinked back tears, and wished Jack were with me to feel the warmth and sense of community. Maybe our rental would become our long-term home.

I reached into my purse to take a picture of the cake, and remembered to ask my hostess.

"Snap away," she said, "before the kids destroy it."
Both Jack and my sister Carolyn would be pleased.

My joy was dimmed by the sight of Anna Butler, seated alone on the back patio, while Charles was in the center of a circle of neighbors, gesturing like a boxer, animated while expressing himself.

After cutting the cake amid snapping cell phones, I walked a piece out to the patio and sat across from Anna.

"Charles doesn't like me to eat sugar," she said, while attempting to smile.

I restrained myself from commenting, hoping she would elaborate.

"He doesn't like belly fat," she said, while patting her skeletal torso, under her dress.

Carolyn would diagnose me as missing my job as a psychologist, but I retained the blank look I had with my patients, as I tried to draw Anna out.

When she offered nothing further, I said, "I saw Charles inside."

"Charles doesn't like me to be around other men," she said, as if she were mentioning a sale at Macy's. As if the comment were innocuous and normative, as one of my colleagues was fond of saying.

"Are you comfortable with that, Anna?"

"Why wouldn't I be?" She asked, looking at me directly for the first time.

"I'm Kim," I said, ready to extricate myself from this strange woman.

"Yes. Your name is on the cake," she said, and I started to wonder if she were one beer short of a six-pack, as my cousin Aidan would say.

"And your husband let you come alone?" She asked.

Dying to call Carolyn, yet again, I said, "Yes, Anna, He did."

The interaction soured me, making the potluck something I had to endure, rather than enjoy. Every time I heard a burst of laughter in the vicinity of Charles, I lost my appetite, knowing my hostess was checking to see if I was trying the assorted dishes.

Sensing she was a romantic, I pulled Katie Dowling into the kitchen and told her I had a surprise for Jack, and needed to leave.

"Enjoy," she said, with genuine warmth.

She fixed me to-go food in Tupperware containers, which I promised to return during the week.

I waved good-bye to the neighbors, thanking them for their welcome. I let myself stare at Charles wanting him to know he may have an audience. He narrowed his eyes, a hint of menace clouding his features.

The Dowling children distracted me, as they each handed me a small gift, and I shook their outstretched hands, smiled, thanked them, and left.

Thrown by my encounter with Charles, I was relieved when the timer lights Jack installed popped on in our new home. So eager was he to excel in his new position, he revved up his natural thoughtfulness in little things, to make our transition easier.

Feeling safe as I entered, I was determined to be rid of the feelings that horrible man brought out in me. What business of it was mine if a long marriage was alien to me? If Anna enjoyed her servitude.

I popped open a beer, and settled into our living room, channel surfing for something funny. I found a Seinfeld re-run and it worked its magic on me, until I heard Jack's voice and bounced up to greet him.

His enthusiasm about his new position was infectious, and we enjoyed a special evening together. When he asked me about the party, I edited the negatives, my obsession with Anna, my revulsion with Charles. Never had a cake received such rave reviews.

A few days later, after washing my neighbor Katie's containers, I decided to drop by, hoping to seem more friendly than I was at the end of the party. The light green buds on the maple trees were sprouting, along with the pink azalea bushes during my short walk to her front door. I tapped gently, and she opened the door quickly.

With a glint in her eye, she said, "I hope our loss was Jack's gain the other night."

"It was, Katie."

Closing the door behind her, she threw up her hands and said, "Kids! What can I tell you? My house is a mess. Kim, we've started a community vegetable plot on Rider Street around the corner. It's our first year. Who knows what it will produce? Please join us. Most of us make a point of being there Thursday mornings so we can catch up. So far, none of the guys are interested."

Sensing a friendship forming, I told Katie I planned to drop by Blair Nursery to pick up some seeds and some gardening tips. And I did just that before picking up a roasted chicken, one of Jack's favorites.

Still feeling a little like a party crasher, I hesitated when I approached the gardening plot on Thursday morning. I recognized a few of the women from the Dowling party, and was ridiculously pleased to see Anna Butler digging in the dirt. After greeting the women, I knelt across from Anna, and using my trowel, began to plant some seeds. After a few minutes of digging, Anna turned to Katie and said, "Charles loves tomatoes. I started them inside six weeks ago. He only eats red ones, so I hope these are red and juicy."

"Anna, Charles will love your tomatoes," Katie said.

Katie's response was so heartfelt, her eyes crinkling with joy, I felt as if I may have the wrong idea about Anna. Maybe I was lacking in wifely devotion....Maybe Jack was missing out on something from me.

Feeling as if Anna would be more open to Katie, I asked Katie if she would consider the three of us walking here together, and then, red-faced with adolescent angst, I withdrew the offer.

"I'll ask her, Kim," Katie said, her lips drawn in an anxious line.

At that moment, I knew Katie was on to Charles and the situation.

Lying with Jack that evening, he noticed the change in me.

"You're getting to like it here, Kim.....the ladies....I mean women....the gardening. I'll quit this job tomorrow if you're not happy. "

"And we'll live on my non income?' I said, knowing it was stupid as soon as I said it.

I made sure his eyes met mine when I told him how much his saying that meant. And that I was making friends and loved digging in the dirt.

A month into our walks to the plot, Anna was smiling and even teasing a bit with Katie. Her husband may have warned her about me, after our non verbal sparring at the potluck dinner. But he obviously had not proclaimed an edict that she avoid me.

And one day, when she saw me working in my own little garden, she called over to me, "Kim, enjoy yourself!"

I felt as if her sense of inclusion with the neighbors had opened her, as it had opened me.

My sister Carolyn felt the move had thrown me off kilter and the RX for me was a job. Maybe in the mix, was her early motherhood's interfering with her education. But she had a profound respect for my degree and profession.

"I need this break, Carolyn. Jack's doing well, and we planned I'd give myself some time to unwind. Taking on peoples' stuff is draining."

"I hear you," she said, able to let go of her own opinions.

En route to our gardening plot, I mentioned Carolyn's feelings about my working to Katie and Anna.

Anna spoke so quietly, we barely heard her.

Katie spoke up, and asked Anna what she had said.

"Charles would never let me work," she said, looking down, knowing it would bother us.

Months ago, at the Dowling dinner, she didn't seem to get how bizarre her comments about him were. If she were one of my patients, I would have noted her embarrassment as growth. I tried to catch Katie's eye, but she rapidly changed the subject, clearly not wishing to gang up on Anna.

But during one of the following Thursdays in the garden, Katie met my eyes when Anna remained silent, looked drawn and gaunt, the slight luster in her cheeks fading, her progress appearing to reverse.

I sensed that Katie may be ready to speak about the situation honestly.

That afternoon, Katie answered my text, and surrounded by her animated children, we sat drinking iced tea in her kitchen. Her kids endeared me to them, as they were as natural and delightful as their mom.

Katie excused herself to put on one of the kids' favorite recordings, which had blasts of noise and plenty of action.

"They rarely listen, but will, if they sense our mood," she said, as she settled back down in the latticed kitchen chair.

"To be honest, Kim, knowing you are a psychologist makes me afraid to say something stupid or out of it. But truth be told, when the Butlers moved in these kids," with a quick thumb point toward the noisy playroom, "were babies, and I slogged around here craving sleep and paying no attention to the neighbors. Nobody warned me how much work kids could be."

"Well, obviously a job well done, Katie," I said, surprising myself with my affection for them.

"Thanks, Kim, she said as she put her finger to her lips, went to the arch in her kitchen and shot a glance into the playroom to ensure our conversation was private.

"I noticed how you reached out to Anna at the potluck which sparked my idea of including you in the veggie garden where we get to know our neighbors."

"In my practice, I've learned to trust gut feelings, and I felt an eerie feeling when Jack and I pulled into our rental. I didn't voice it, as I knew Jack had chosen it, and we try to be good to one another.....always."

"Yes, we do too, but I know what you see in Anna's deference to Charles is different than that," Katie said solemnly.

"Do we have grounds for an intervention?" I asked her, hoping for a yes.

"There is no battery, and no proof of any kind of verbal abuse...so, no, I think we just try to befriend her," Katie said kindly.

I left Katie's that Thursday afternoon feeling that Katie's life was so rich with her family, she didn't have as much room as I to dwell on strange neighbors. But I did, and I wanted a chance to untangle Anna's knots to help her to blossom. But my instincts told me I wouldn't get that chance.

The Thursday before the 4th of July, Anna wasn't in front of her house, and I went directly to Katie's. We both thought it was odd, as Anna had taken to texting Katie occasionally, if she was unable to attend a neighborhood event.

Katie reminded me that Charles was out of town on business, and maybe Anna had joined him. My gut told me that wasn't the case. That Charles would not allow it.

After a poor night's sleep, I couldn't shake the sense that something was wrong with Anna, and that I should follow my instincts and investigate.

Shortly after Jack left for work, I decided to stop by the Butlers' household.

After ringing the bell, and knocking, I turned the door knob, and found it was open.

Her home was very quiet. I stood in the foyer breathing deeply, and calling her name.

"Anna, it's Kim. Are you home?"

Knowing her bedroom was on the first floor, I inched along the hallway.

I felt her, before I saw her.

She looked peaceful; she looked sad; as she lay there lifeless, a note by her side.

I screamed and started to go to Katie's, but called her instead.

My years of watching crime shows helped me resist the urge to touch her, or read her note. There is a blank in my mind of what happened in the minutes before the police arrived.

I will always remember the expression on Officer Wilson's face, when I asked him to read me the note, and his "Sorry, Ma'am, it's personal...to the husband. Seems she disappointed him," the catch in his voice grounding me to the realization, that he was as upset as I. That his work had not blunted him. That he knew some people were too timid for this life, and we should notice them, show the courage to reach out to help them, to show them their strength ......while they are still among us.

From: Scarlet Leaf Review

DR. McGILL

Jenny pushed my newspaper aside. She held her pen in the air waiting for my input. We were planning a joint birthday party. I hesitated confiding in her about the bomb that just exploded. My Mom sent me the local paper. Jenny and I shared an apartment an hour from home. Mom rarely pushed herself on me, and I was touched by her sending the paper.

It was on the third page. " Local pediatrician arrested for battery." Finally, I thought.

Dr. Mc Gill played golf with my dad. Mrs. McGill and my mom were friends.

"Meghan, what's going on?" Jenny said, no longer interested in her party list.
She sat up, scraping the chair as she straightened her shoulders.

"Your parents are friends of the McGills, right?" I said, deciding what to say.

" Not like yours. My dad works so much, and mom hangs out with her sisters."

" Jen, do you have some time, or are you in a hurry?"

"No. No plans. What is it, Meghan?"

And so I started to share a story locked deeply within. My pediatrician, Dr. McGill abused me, repeatedly. Not in a sexual way. A sadistic, tricky way. A pinch here, an arm bend there. It didn't happen every visit, or I think I would have told my mother. Just when I started to relax about doctor visits, I'd feel the pinch in my bicep, the fingers hurting my jaw.

In the way that children know their parents secrets, I knew dad's being a member of the club was a big deal. I've also perfected the art of eavesdropping, since I could make sense of the words my parents spoke to each other. It was comforting how gentle the sounds were, so unlike the stories in the after school specials....words like bitch thrown around with poor attempts to dub them. I also knew my being an only child was not my mom's idea. My father wanted me to have everything he didn't have as a child. Seeing me sign a slip for a hot dog at the club, put my father close to rapture.

Dad had learned to restrain himself from his caddy stories; working in the heat, his shoulder pain, his counting his earnings with one of his sisters. In our earlier home, in an average neighborhood, my dad was more honest about his family's meager resources.All that changed with the move. When Dr. McGill left my skin or jaw sore, I couldn't bear to ruin things for my parents.

Mom grew up signing for lunch, so the club was just a place to her, not a destination.

My first visit to Dr. McGill scared me because I was afraid of needles. My mother filled out paperwork and the nurse did what nurses do - measured my height and weight, took my temperature and asked me a few questions. I remember Mom reading a magazine in a corner of the exam room. The handsome doctor shook my hand, and made me feel like an adult.

"No needles, today?" I asked him.

"We're just getting you set up for visits," he said.

I noticed little specks of white in his dark hair as I leaned my head back with that thing on my tongue. I remember a lot about what happened in our new fancy neighborhood. Nothing about Dr. McGill creeped me out that first day. I learned to read my mother's reactions early in life, and I could tell she was happy to get me settled with a new doctor.

"Meghan, I can tell you aren't ready to share most of this," Jenny said quietly. I realized I had said very few words to her, and was mostly reflecting on the past. I definitely didn't want to share anything about my father's need for social status.

"Jen, do whatever you need to do. I appreciate your being here, but I've repressed so much, I don't know how to put it.

Jenny, an avid runner, pulled her hair into a scrunchie, hugged me, and left me to sort through my memories.

The first memory that popped up was his squeezing my thigh tightly during an exam. He had just done that knee- kick thing, and asked me to look into a light he held. My thigh felt pain, but I figured he was the doctor, and there must be a reason for things. Later that night, I remember bluish marks on my upper right leg. I felt it all afternoon and saw it when I put on my favorite nightgown. I didn't say anything about it, and put it out of my mind until the time he pushed on my jaw. Then I knew there was something evil about Dr. McGill.

Seated comfortably in my apartment, the power of these memories threatened to ruin my sanctuary. Jen and I had chosen our decor with affection. Each piece delighted us, and reflected our tastes, quirks and all. We received tables and dishes from our parents, but we needed the place to feel like us. We had maintained a friendship through high school and college, failed and thriving romances, and a few drunken keg parties. It was our first apartment after college, and neither of us had found the dream job in our field. We were both slinging hash in restaurants, making our home a chalice for our dreams.

Jenny returned from her run with a bag from Bagel Bin, little smeared spots seeping through the white bag. Ever fastidious in her diet, I knew the kindness in that little bag. Also, she wanted to hear about Dr. McGill. And I wanted to tell her.

"One of the scariest times was a pool party at the McGill's," I said, smearing creamed cheese on my raison bagel. I hoped my prepping distracted Jen from my inability to enjoy it right now.

"I heard about them. Dr. McGill donning his chef's cap, flipping steaks, sipping martinis. I think my parents were jealous they didn't make the cut for those," Jen said.

"You were lucky.... Jen,... the man was a monster. The martinis were more for show. Even as a little kid, I knew a drinker from a drunk. Jenny, I hadn't thought of this one until today. Your run gave me time to face some of this stuff. "

"Bagel Bin is not on my route," Jen said, glancing at my uneaten treat. "I'm sorry, Meghan. It's not about me. Tell me about the pool party."

"The bastard tried to drown me!"

"Get out! How did he get away with it?*

"How did he get away with any of it? Jen."

"It was late afternoon, and we were playing Marco Polo, quietly. We knew to keep our voices down. Dr. Mc Gill eased into the water. Heads were bobbing "Marco," "Polo," and I felt a hand holding my head down until I struggled to break free. Jen, it was a bunch of really popular kids, and I didn't want to miss out, so I let it happen more than once."

"Ashley Baxter's crowd?"

"I don't remember who, but they weren't worth dying over."

I then told Jen about the hate in his eyes as I looked up through the water, pleading for mercy with my eyes. When he released me, his teeth were big, his smile malicious. It was our last encounter, as I insisted on going to my parents' doctor. Still protecting my dad, I remember making a big adolescent rant about being too mature for a kid's doctor. The details are foggy, but I know I was never in his company again.

And now this. It was time to take a stand against him, if I were needed.

Our land line rang and I checked the caller ID. It was my mom.

"Meghan, did you see that story about Joe McGill?"

Wanting time to think, I pretended I hadn't seen it.

"Mom, Jen just brought home bagels, and I'm about to read the paper you sent. I love getting it. Thanks for sending. What's up?"

"Meghan, people will do anything these days. They're saying Joe abused kids. Can you imagine?"

Knowing my mother could read me, even from afar, I needed to explode a bomb of my own. "Mom. I will drive down to see you and dad soon, and we'll talk about everything," I said. Confident in her affection, I knew a visit from me would dispel all other thoughts from her mind.

"Hank, I mean Dad and I were just saying it's been a while since we saw you, Meghan. When will you arrive?"

"Mom, I just thought of it now. Maybe this weekend if I can get my shifts covered."

The dead silence that followed reminded me not to mention my job. I made the little circular finger motion to Jen to call my cell. She did, and I told Mom I'd get back to her soon. Needed to take this call.

"Meghan, I never thought you'd ask for the cell phone bit with your mom. "

She guided me to our comfy couch and handed me a pillow to hug, our ritual in tough times. "I overheard you tell your mother you'd visit soon. Maybe I'll join you. Go see my family."

"I'd be happy to drive, unless you'd need a car at home," I said.

"We'll work out the details, but first we have to get our shifts covered."

Jenny leaned back on the couch, stretching her long legs under the coffee table.

"Meghan, the statute of limitations on most crimes is short. Except for murder. Think about how far you want to go with this thing, before you do anything. I haven't seen you like this since your break-up with Justin."

"That bad?"

"This is pretty lame, but I always thought Dr. McGill was a creep," Jen said, as she got up and did the full leg stretches she must have missed after her run. She got back down on the couch and turned to me. "All of this of this is off the record till you decide what to do. Let's get our shifts covered and ride home together this weekend."

Neither of us could find subs for Sunday brunch, so we decided to drive home Thursday. Jenny could borrow her brother's truck to get around town.

After working lunch Thursday, we packed my SUV with enough clothes for a cruise on the Seine. Jen's eyes caught mine, as we loaded the trunk. "One thing I don't miss about Justin. By now there would be a lecture to pack lightly. 'Meghan, five pairs of shoes?' "

We had perfected the route with the least rush-hour traffic for our jaunts home. The moon was bright, and as round as a plate. Jenny Googled it, and found it was due to be full tomorrow. We spoke no further of Dr. McGill, enjoying the quiet of a long friendship.

After I dropped Jenny off, I opened the windows and sang. As I turned into Mystic Cove, Officer Jackson stepped out of the gate house to see me. I got out of my car. "Beverly," I said, my cheek brushing her name plate, "So good to see you. I'm surprising them, so please don't call."

They knew I was coming, but thought it was tomorrow. If they were out, I was free to let myself in with my key. I parked up the street next to the bench, book-ended with sculptured angels. Figuring they would be out back, I made my way there, having left my bags in the car. My mother's voice was shrill. "Hank, you knew?"

"Marcie, I didn't know, I just heard things."

"When he was still Meghan's doctor?"

"I didn't believe the rumors, Marcie."

"Oh, Hank...Our little girl. If there were any truth..."

I then heard the first slammed door in my home, my mother too furious to speak.

I tip-toed back to the bench to give myself time to calm down. A cloud passed over the moon, as I thought of the fiction of my life, the fiction of my father's protection. As I looked at a fountain near a putting green, I knew my mom would have collided a few planets if she had known, the force of her love propelling me to my trunk, to get my things, and visit my parents.

From: Potluck Magazine

THE STEEL DOOR

Twelve guards. I counted. The new guy puts my feet in cloth
shoes. Nobody smiles. I shuffle my shackled feet to the steel door.
They open it and lead me to the gurney in the box cage. It buzzes
as it goes backward. The big needle is the last thing I see before I
close my eyes.

From: Indicia Literary Journal

THE INVITATION

It was mid afternoon when I saw it on the table. A thick egg-shelled envelope engraved with our names. Henry was visiting his mother, and Stella had lifted her umbrella from the ornate stand. " Mrs. Palmer, I left dinner instructions next to the fridge."

"Thank you, Stella," I said, thinking Henry would enjoy an outing after his visit, probably filet with a musky cabernet. Whenever I fiddled in the kitchen, Henry's face looked drawn and wistful. He needed to get things right with me, and to shelter me from harm. How this involved my cooking, I had no idea. Maybe an episode with his mother, or his ex - wife I thought. It was deeper than my not being gourmet.

We had met in a continuing education class at the local high school. We were sharpening our skills in the French language, both of us rusty from non use. The teacher was a lively woman from Geneva, her hands delicate and expressive, as if conducting an orchestra.
Few of us missed her class, finding in her a spark of child-like delight.

I noticed Henry during the first evening class, his tweed jacket so classic, the lines of his jaw pronounced. But it was when I felt his notice that I was captured, a sliver of hope that he felt the same way.

It was a mild May evening when Henry spoke to me. I had imagined it so many times, that I was mute when he spoke, thinking it another daydream. My car was covered in light green fluff from the budding maples. "Eileen," he said, "I have a brush for your car." A beginning so practical. so Henry-like, but I didn't know that yet. After a moment's delay, I thanked him and watched him go to his car, after tilting his head toward it.

How does he know my name?, I thought, stupidly forgetting how often Madame used it in class. .I reminded myself to thank him simply, offering no apology, acting, if not feeling, as if I deserved his attention.

The trance was broken by a former student. "Miss Mc Bride, you back here?" as he screeched his bike to a halt near us. "Evening school, Dylan. I'm a student," wishing I had given him those detentions I hadn't. Henry gave him one of those looks I came to know, and Dylan cycled away.

It was Maureen whom I called, the most romantic of my sisters.

"He's not married, is he?" she said, after her initial joy.

"I doubt it, " I said savoring the way he brushed my arm.

Soon after that night, there were many more encounters. At a candle-lit dinner Henry ordered a vintage year cabernet, and I had to admit that I don't drink, and he tilted his head as if to say, Why not? Whether or not he shared that with his mother rattled me from time to time. Meeting his mother didn't go smoothly.. There were covert references to Barbara, whom I knew by then, was Henry's first wife.

When I refused a cocktail, Jean Palmer's eyes widened slightly, sparking my imagination of what Henry may have shared about my problem. There was a flicker of amusement in her expression, as she rose to offer me something else. Even back then, with my insecurities about my tribe, I had to admit she gracefully switched gears, and presented me with Canada Dry ginger ale.

Mrs. Palmer, as I thought of her, long after assuming the name myself, had a special skill in evoking my neuroses. I remember an early summer afternoon on her patio, sparkling water in hand, when her closest friend asked me if I had a brother or sister. Was the question cordial and innocent? Probably. But there was no mistaking the friend's intake of breath, when I answered that I had three of each.

How could I feel shame about any of them? Katie with her thick auburn hair and generous heart; Danny, with his silly jokes after painting with Daddy in the blistering sun?

Had I subconsciously chosen this crowd to prolong the self-torture? One look at Henry reading, sleeping, attempting to dance, and I told Jung and Freud to go to hell. I loved Henry Palmer and knew he loved me. But any time spent with his family and friends reduced me to ethnic self-loathing and wincing when they said " Eileen."

I began to attach ridiculous importance to the invitation we received to the wedding. Jay, Henry's prep school buddy, invited us to his son J.D.'s wedding. Henry had lost touch with him for years, but a mutual friend had given him our address. A liberal arts major like myself, I pictured Jay and I bonding over Proust or Shakespeare, silly pompous daydreams that frittered away my time, causing Stella to repeat her deferential requests. "Mrs. Palmer, may I mop the kitchen floor now?"

At times, I wanted to tell Stella to chill with the formal stuff, call me Eileen, and maybe hang out and download a movie with me. But I knew that the caste system that had thoroughly screwed with my head would not allow it. Would the earth go off - kilter if two women forgot the rules and had some fun? Probably not, but my wiring wasn't that of a pioneer.

When my head was spinning with these thoughts, I called my sister Katie. I told her about the wedding invitation, and voiced some feelings about it.

'Eileen, you've got to clear your head of this stuff."

Uh oh, I thought.

"Mother and Daddy worked hard to educate us.

We can hold our own with anybody.

Where did you get this serf mentality?"

I smarted at her response and envied her sure-footedness. I asked about her kids, and we went back and forth naturally, few signs of a ripple between us. It was like that with my sisters. All of them.

The following day, I blew off steam on the elliptical at Gold's, feeling foolish for voicing the garbage in my head. I chastised myself for holding on to hang-ups about pedigree. Who cares if Daddy wasn't a Yalie like Barbara's Dad? Certainly not

Henry. Not given to outbursts, Henry would redden from the collar up, when he re-enacted the scene at The Halfway House, between him and ole Chester. The name of the ninth hole bistro bothered me in ways I chose not to voice.

I left Gold's feeling saucy and excited about cleaning up and choosing a dress for the wedding. Henry noticed when I wore black, sometimes whispering about my fair skin, leaving me to question his taste, rather than tasting his ardor.

The scent of barbecue chicken mingled with the odor of floor cleanser, as I made my way into the kitchen.

"One of Mr. Palmer's favorites," Stella said, pointing to the crock pot, her joy in pleasing him a constant in our lives. " He just called to ask what I've made him," so besotted with Henry, she saw no insult in excluding me. Not that she was a big fan of Barbara's. She adopted a pinched look if her name came up, and actually volunteered that Barbara... sniffed as SHE... didn't like her pecan pie.

"If Mr. Palmer calls again, please tell him I've gone shopping," I said, visualizing the slinky black dress I would wear to J.D.'s wedding.

When I entered Becker's Dress Shop, I heard Ginny Sawyer's imperious snarl enunciating her displeasure with the selection. I tried to escape her notice, but stumbled into a swinging rack of dresses.

Ginny didn't fool me. She was familiar to me on a cellular level. Put simply, she knew fear although she chose to go on offense to dispel it. My M. O. was more defensive.

" Colleen," she called out. Becker's Dress was not the site to correct her, yet again, about my name.

" Ginny, it's been a while."

" Oh, I'm sure that dreamy Henry Palmer is keeping you busy," she said, disarming me a bit, but not the saleswoman, her face crimson with offended restraint.

I was reminded that Ginny's moods vacillated, even when sober. Henry steered me away from her when choosing our table at Gravers Lane Inn. I remember her smoky voice rolling across the cocktail bar, the evening we met. Introduced to me as a friend of Henry's ex, Ginny was nearly as smitten with Henry as was our housekeeper Stella, which oddly, warmed me to her.

But my warmth was short-lived when I overheard her describing me to a few friends, her voice thick with cosmopolitans. " Freckle-faced, buxom little thing, his Colleen." Not the worst thing to overhear, but the sense of my other-ness slurred through.

Smiling at Ginny, I backed out of Becker's Dress and headed for the mall. Tempted by the aromas of the food court, I headed to Bloomingdale's to find the perfect dress for J.D.'s wedding. Henry, like most men, had little interest in the event, but since the arrival of the invitation, I had allowed a manic-like intensity to consume me. I reminded myself to alert him to the date, so I could meet so many friends of his from his younger days.

He was in the library, organizing his book shelves when I crept by with a dress that would have raised an eyebrow from my mother. His concentration during every task was so endearing , complementing my cluttered mind. I was relieved Stella had left for the day, and after I modeled the dress for him, I was able to break his concentration.

The following day, I nearly slipped on Stella's newly waxed floor, thanking my yoga practice for keeping my balance. I checked myself from scolding her for not warning me, as "Mr. Palmer" was her universe. The irony that I thought of it as Stella's floor, and not my own, struck me, as I grabbed the black granite ledge of the sink.

The episode kept me from babbling like a school girl to Stella about my new dress. Face it, my sisters were sick of my schtick, and didn't quite see what I saw in Henry in the first place.

Just after re-gaining my balance, the land line rang and I answered it.

" Eileen, this is Jean Palmer. How are you?" she said.

" Good. And you?" stopping myself from calling her Mrs. Palmer.

" Is Stella available?"

" She's just leaving. I'll get her, Mrs. Palmer," I said, slipping back.

It wasn't my fault, as the Jean thing was new.

With my special skill in eavesdropping, I deduced that Stella would accompany Mrs. Palmer to the wedding that was the source of my frenzy. Henry's mother no longer drove, and she felt comfortable with Stella. Maybe it was my imagination, but the deference Stella showed to anyone Palmer, elevated her status in the family.

I placed a red circle on the calendar in Henry's study, marking the date of the wedding. Imagining my mother making a guest appearance, I went back to the mall and purchased a shawl to wrap around my shoulders should the dress feel too slight.

The morning of the wedding was one of October's best - a crispness in the air and the leaves like golden rust. I wondered if the bride had chosen this date knowing it's beauty would make the day of her vows more precious. I scolded myself for having given the bride and groom so little thought.

The parents of the groom were chatting in the foyer of the Episcopal church.

Jay strode over to us, and actually hugged Henry.

"Let's not lose one another again," he said to Henry, while releasing him.

Henry introduced me to Jay and his wife Ellen who was restrained in her greeting.

However, I noticed throughout the service that she remained poised and erect, her shoulders back, her tiny waist showing the mother of the groom dress like a petite model giving boring taupe a second look.

Throughout the service, I peeked at the crowd assembled and saw that one of the few people I knew was Ginny Sawyer.

Stella would be bringing Mrs. Palmer directly to the reception.

The bride's appearance surprised me. As Kristen's father, teary-eyed and endearing, escorted her up the aisle, I noticed she was athletic-looking and muscular, not the slender looking waif I had imagined. J.D., whom I had yet to meet, was beaming at the altar, assuring me that this was a happy event.

After meeting the bride and groom, and many of Henry's old friends, I began to relax into the event, kicking myself for my hang-ups about not being Barbara or of the Ivy League set.
The reception was tasteful with fresh flowers on every table, making a lovely contrast with the white table cloths. There was a

choice of entrees, and the band's music was gentle and not over-bearing as is the case with many weddings.

While dancing with Henry, I began to feel that my dress was a bit revealing, so I headed to the coat room in the foyer to retrieve my shawl. There was nobody there to help me, so I fumbled through the jackets to find it.

It was Ginny's voice that stopped me from moving. She was articulating each syllable to hide her consumption, but I heard every slurred word.

"Bet that little tart has you missing Barbara," she said.

I feared I would explode from holding my breath, thankful for the slight screech of a wheelchair.

" Ginny, Eileen is a fine woman, and she loves my son. You should behave more like her," Mrs. Palmer said.

I waited alone in the coat room, choking back tears of joy and shame. How had I given so much power to the Palmers? Memories from my childhood surfaced....Daddy in his Santa suit that never fit...Danny whistling at us when we dressed for the prom....Riches from my youth that were more than enough to sustain me.

Touched by Jean Palmer's endorsement, I realized I didn't need it, and probably never had.

Henry peeked into the coat room.

"Eileen, I missed you," he said.

Leaving the shawl under one of the coats, I took his hand and asked him to dance.

From: Phoenix Photo & Fiction

CHARLOTTE'S WORLD

Charlotte Evans was a fifty year old bartender. "Whiskey on the rocks" Frankie said, as he adjusted the sound on the remote. "Did your ears get shot off on duty?" Charlotte asked him as she added ice to his drink. " My pension doesn't say anything about hearing loss, Charlie,"

The ritual was well established. Frankie would use the nickname she hated, and play the role of tough ex cop. He had been a cop, but he faked the tough.

Tom arrived and Charlotte placed his beer at his spot before he sat down. Some guests wanted their drinks without asking. Others did not.

" I felt like I hit a grand slam in the bottom of the thirteenth, first pension check I got," Frankie told Tom and the couple at the high top behind him. Any hearing person in his vicinity heard about Frankie's pension.

Since Rocco's arrival, Charlotte preferred anything Frankie said to Rocco's comments. "Broad's too old for this place." " She must be giving the house away...Why else would they come?" The owner hired Rocco to spy on long time employees, like Charlotte. He counted the cash drawers often, making sure no money was pilfered by her or the other bartenders. His was also the job of watching to see that the regulars didn't get that extra drizzle of brew or spirit.

Making sure the busboys emptied a trash can or two should be his job, Charlotte thought. The patrons walked to the bar in the city, lending little harm to Charlotte's topping off here and there. Soot-stained overalls made their way to see her before the trudge to their row houses or apartments. She felt respected by the guys who worked with their bodies, laying bricks or painting roofs. A few offered Rocco a short trip outside when he uttered a rough remark about her. They also understood that their tips were her paycheck.

Charlotte had worked in fancy clubs where the guests signed for her service, often leaving her struggling to pay her rent on time. She felt at home with Frankie and Tom, and most of her regulars. She also felt his presence, the little face, no bigger than an orange, who arrived in a hospital three blocks from here, thirty years ago.

She allowed her parents to influence her decision to let him go, not knowing the price of such a loss. Each year since, most keenly the day in July, punctuated with fireworks, Charlotte grieved the loss of her son. Having given up on his interest in finding her, she felt comfort working close to the site of his arrival.

"Those rocks glasses aren't going to wash themselves, Lady" Rocco said just when the owner stopped by to check out the place. She really didn't fear the owner as she had out-lasted too many managers to count. But she could feel herself coloring and turning from her visitors, ignoring Rocco while he sauntered by.

"She's home spending my pension. Home Shopping thing on TV," Frankie told the couple to his left. Charlotte noticed Frankie's failure to charm. Unusual.

The clatter coming from the restaurant caught everyone's attention.

"Man down! Call 911!"

Servers gathered around a booth. Charlotte came out from behind the bar. Rocco's fists were pounding the chest of a hulk of a man, and Charlotte rushed over to help him. She reached under Rocco's fists and took over the chest thumping.
Rocco gave her a break, just when the stretcher arrived banging into a dessert cart, spilling some gooey contents onto the floor.

Rocco. kneeling beside the booth, locked eyes with Charlotte. "Nice work, Charlotte." She noticed he called her by name.

Frankie helped them up. "Force could of used you two. Saved the sucker's life."

The sucker played high school football with Rocco. Played better than Rocco. Got a partial scholarship to Michigan and played until he blew out his knee in junior year. Charlotte learned all this at the end of her shift. Rocco had closed the place after the episode, amidst complaints from the servers that he was starving their children or keeping Pebbles from the vet. The young ones, living with their parents, took their freedom out back, stinking up the dumpster area with the strong smell of weed.

Frankie asked Charlotte to join the fellows for a drink. She stared him down better than many of his perps. "The big guy wants you there," Frankie whispered to her, his breathe smelling of the cigarette he stepped outside to smoke. Good thing Frankie's not near the dumpster, Charlotte thought. Her hands were trembling as she poured a draft beer to join the men at the bar.

Tom and Frankie provided the buffer she needed. One life-saving CPR session didn't wash away the ill will she felt for her boss. But Frankie had a way with her that she couldn't resist. He also knew about the little treasure she had given up that summer, long ago.

"Where'd you learn CPR?" Rocco leaned forward on the bar to see past the guys.
"I have a life, Rocco." Charlotte hoped he could picture her sipping wine in an evening dress, hitting tennis balls at he club, or even playing cards with friends.

"Charlotte isn't married to this place, Rocco. My buddies who guard the hospital told me your buddy came through O.K. Hooked up like an octopus but gonna make it" Her actual name uttered twice in one evening. Did emergencies soften people?

Her hands still trembling, she listened to the football stories around her.
The blocking that Rocco and Matt did, so the running backs could weave their figure eights to the goal line. "He was better than me though...stood out enough to get him to Michigan" Rocco told the guys.

Knowing she was not expected to talk football gave Charlotte the chance to imagine her son bobbing and weaving down the field. Maybe a quarterback, lean and quick-witted like her Dad. Or a musician with long fingers massaging piano keys, or strumming a guitar. Or maybe he became a teacher, inspiring students, planting memories in them when their hearts were open, in harmony with life. When her fantasies took her to images of his being a junkie or a thief, she grabbed a bar rag and began to wipe it clean.

She realized she had forgotten to clock out of her shift. No more time cards in a clunky basement machine. She had to go back to the computer to punch in her worker number. The guys continued to tell their war stories. The episode had rocked them all. Before Charlotte grabbed her jacket to walk home, she took the bar rag over to the gooey spot on the floor next to the dessert cart. Rocco said, "I've got it, Charlotte."

Awakened by a noisy truck, Charlotte fixed herself a cup of instant coffee. While trying to read the paper, she felt distracted and restless. She decided to call City Hospital to check on her patient. Rocco had referenced his last name in some of his tales. Before placing the call, Charlotte checked the adoption website, a habit as natural to her as breathing.

The harried hospital phone operator put her on hold, coming back on the line with a room number and a condition: stable. Rarely impulsive, Charlotte surprised herself. She decided to visit Matt Wilson. Although she would prefer to wear her sneakers, she chose her dressy black slacks and shoes. She didn't know why she was doing this, but it felt right.

She boarded a bus for the short trip remembering to bring the exact change. She chose a seat in the front, next to a man in a business suit, his face tight, his lips pinched together. A stench of garbage entered through the electronic double doors. Charlotte looked through the wide windows in the front of the bus and saw they were behind a city garbage truck.

Regretting her outfit, she knew she could get to the hospital quicker in her sneakers and jeans. At least I won't miss my stop, Charlotte thought as the garbage truck rumbled along in front of them. The streets were too narrow for the bus to advance.

She looked past the man beside her to see two spiked-hair teenaged boys approaching an elderly woman, her purse clutched tightly to her chest. They pointed to the light and stopped her from advancing into traffic, then continued on their way, their baggy jeans hanging loosely on their skinny butts.

The bus driver announced the stops in advance of his pulling over to the curb.

"City Hospital next" he said as she felt her stomach rumble as the bus pulled right in front of the entrance. The building was large and imposing. She nearly froze in her seat as the bus driver repeated "City Hospital. One stop only" She got up from her seat and descended the steps of the bus and walked into the lobby.

A blast of cold air hit her as she walked over to the large oval desk marked Visitors.
"License, please." the young woman behind the desk said, looking bored and a little hostile. As Charlotte fumbled through her wallet for her license, the woman said "Patient name" and Charlotte straightened her shoulders and said "Matthew Wilson" as if she and Matt were good friends. The receptionist looked at the license, then up at her, and wrote Charlotte Evans on a sticky name tag. She handed the tag to Charlotte, all of her stubby fingers adorned with rings, her wrists jingling with bangle bracelets. "Room 404. Go left"

In striking contrast to the sullen receptionist, Charlotte was greeted by a perky teenager, a hospital volunteer, to escort her to the elevator. Double doors swooshed open for them and she nearly gagged on the antiseptic odor of the hospital corridor, barely concealing the scent of sweat and urine. The youngster appeared immune from scents, bouncing along with her golden curls like cork screws swaying down to her waist. Another set of doors and they were back in the lobby area. " I'm new." Carlie said. Charlotte didn't mind the detour as she felt nervous and ridiculous for visiting this stranger.

When the elevator stopped on the fourth floor, she got out and saw the signs directing her to the lower numbers, Room 404. Having the detour prepared her for the peculiar hospital scents. She squared her shoulders and approached the room, her heels clicking along the hard floors. Rm. 404 Wilson, M., the name stuck into the plastic holder.

Not quite an octopus, Charlotte thought as she peeked into the private room. He did have a small tube in his nose extending to a wheeled machine with a screen next to him. He noticed her instantly, giving her no time to retreat from her fool's mission.

"Mr. Wilson? I'm Charlotte Evans. We met last night at The Beacon."

"That Charlotte? Who helped Rocco? You just missed him" he said as if being pumped back to life were an every day happening. He beckoned her over to shake his hand which was calloused and strong. He gave her a hearty handshake and looked directly into her eyes. Losing his bluster, he bit back his lower lip and said "Thank you. You and Rocco saved my life.'

"Mr. Wilson."

"Matt."

" I can't explain why I'm here, but I'm glad I came. You look pretty good. What are the doctors saying?'

"That I had a heart attack and I'm lucky to be here. But with the right meds, I should be here to meet my grandkids." With that, his wife walked into the room and Charlotte excused herself. After a short introduction, she backed up to leave and Matt said, "Rocco gave you a lot of credit."

Charlotte didn't know if the moon were full or the earth had shifted, but as she made her way out of the hospital, she smiled and looked forward to telling Frankie and Tom about the visit.

When she got home and changed her clothes into her comfortable sweats, she went to the computer. There were still a few hours until her shift at The Beacon began. She browsed the web for new sneakers and wanted to make the one click for them to appear, like magic, at her front door. But she decided to wait and try them on as she spent so much time on her feet.

She answered a few e mails and saw something in her in-box that shook her to her foundation. THIS IS NOT SPAM. Birth mother search confirmation. The subject line of the e mail. She scrolled down and read a short note from someone she had waited thirty years to meet again.

My name is Michael De Lucia. I have been aware of you since I turned eighteen, and have followed your entries on the adoption website. I believe you are my birth mother. My mother died last year, and I needed to respect her feelings about contacting you. I understand that this may upset your life. I do not intend to impose myself on you, but if you would be open to meeting me, I would like to meet you. I want to thank you for giving me life, which has been good so far. My wife, Terry, has been encouraging me to do this.

Sincerely.
Mike De Lucia
P.S. I was born on the Fourth of July.

Charlotte read the message over and over. She grabbed a Coke from her fridge, wanting something stronger, but knowing her shift would start in a few hours. She paced around her apartment, her breath coming in short gasps and gulps. Michael. She spoke the name aloud, liking its' sound. Michael, married to Terry. He was real and he wanted to meet her. She wished she had a sister to call to calm her fears, to enjoy this news, to guide her response. Her own parents, gone for more than a decade, were no longer here to help her. She felt a wave of resentment toward them, especially when she re-read the line about his mother.

The earth had shifted. Charlotte's world had changed. Her son wanted to enter it.

She watered her plants, and rinsed her coffee cup, knowing she was avoiding her response. What if I write the wrong thing? she thought, as she stared straight ahead, her vision blurry with tears. Her work gave her an understanding of men, and how hard it is for them to talk about things that mattered. She owed it to Michael to write back. And she did.

Dear Michael, I have missed you every day. Nothing would make me happier than meeting you. Please let me know where you want me to be. I am so thankful your life has been good.

Sincerely,
Charlotte Evans

Feeling more like herself behind the bar at The Beacon, Charlotte remembered her guests' drink choices. "House red for the lady. Bottled Bud, no glass for the Mr." The couple she was serving hadn't been in for a while, and they both lit up like they had won the lottery when she remembered their drinks. They brightened even more when she asked how their son Thomas liked college.

She left the remote at Frankie's spot at the bar, hoping he would blast the sound so she could share her news without being overheard. All she needed was a stoned server or a useless busboy churning the rumor mill.

True to form, the sound from the television escalated. Charlotte leaned across the bar toward Frankie as she handed him his drink.

"I have big news."

"You went to the hospital to meet the guy. I already know. Just missed you there."

"Yeah, but that's not it. My kid got in touch. Sent me an e-mail. His name is Michael.

Wants to meet me."

"Ah, Charlie. He's gonna love ya."

Finding restraint an over-rated virtue, Frankie shared Charlotte's news with Tom and a few of the regulars. Armed with Michael's full name and date of birth, he even had one of the guys on the force do a background check. Clean. It didn't take Charlotte long to catch on.

"How do you know he's a landscaper? He just told me that today."

"We have to look out for you, Charlie."

Near the service bar, one of the servers was gesturing toward Charlotte. She walked over and a scruffy-looking guy with a nose ring held a colorful basket of flowers. " Last delivery of the day for Charlotte Evans. My boss said to wait until five." She handed him a tip and thanked him.

"Secret admirer?" A man near Frankie said. Charlotte set the lush arrangement on the bar. The golden rust-colored flowers sprouted from the tasteful basket, mixed with daisies and ferns. Charlotte opened the card, read it, and showed it to Frankie. " Matt Wilson and family."

Rocco and a few servers walked over to see the flowers. Frankie showed them the card. Rocco's shoulders sagged as if letting go of hostility, and said. "Good work on Matt, Charlotte."

Charlotte heard but did not see him, as she was busy wiping a spot on the computer, her back to them all.

Charlotte's son was faithful in sending and returning e-mails. He lived in a neighboring suburb, and his busiest work days were toward the weekend. He invited her to dinner at DeMarco's Ristorante, close to The Beacon, the following Tuesday. His love for his father shown through his descriptions of DeLucia Landscaping, which his dad had started before he was twenty. His dad had introduced him to De Marco's for special occasions when he was a little boy.

A stab of pain went through her as she read this. Not only was Michael real, he belonged to the people who raised him. And here she was, a bartender in an apartment, with little to brag about. She combed through her closet looking for an outfit to wear next Tuesday.

Michael knew she worked at The Beacon, so he couldn't expect her to be like the ladies at the club where she once worked, bejeweled, and signing slips of paper for their meals, bemoaning their putting or tennis serve.

A flush of shame crept through her when she realized how petty she was being, begrudging Michael anything. She also felt ungrateful for resenting her job, and her buddies at the bar. Hell, even Rocco was warming up.

Saturday night, three days before DeMarco's, the bar was slammed. Her long time bar back cleaned glasses, worked the service bar, and got the food runners moving to get the meals delivered. Rocco poured a few drinks and dug into the soapy water, his shirt sleeves getting damp and rumpled. Charlotte scooted behind him to get a coke for a new customer. She handed him a menu and told him she'd be right back. He left cash on the bar and disappeared.

Charlotte was so wiped out from the busy shift, she had no trouble sleeping, her nerves calmed by pure exhaustion. Her regulars assured her she'd do fine at The Ristorante.

Tuesday evening, she took a cab to DeMarco's. The host asked her to follow him to meet Mr. De Lucia. He guided her to a large round table. Completely surprised, the first person she noticed was Frankie, dressed in a brown suit and tie. Tom was next to him along with a few of the servers and busboys. She recognized her son in the group. He had ordered the coke from her the other night.. He hugged her and said "I'm Michael. I would have invited Terry if I knew about all this..." he said, clearly relieved by the company. "I've waited a long time for this, Michael," she said her tears flowing freely.

Frankie said, "We will let you two get to know each other, or we can stay and tell you a few good stories, like the time Charlie threw out the owner's brother when she was new."

"Or the night a keg exploded," Tom said.

"How she never once ratted me out to the boss." This, from one of the busboys.

"Stay. I hope to get to know this special lady."

He lifted his glass as he spoke and Charlotte noticed his hands were like her own father's, like one of her fantasies of her son. But he was really here, in Charlotte's world, and she remained quiet, breathing in the gratitude of his forgiveness, and gratitude for the boys from The Beacon.

Her friends from the bar didn't stay after all, and Charlotte and Michael enjoyed a delicious meal together. He didn't ask her why she had given him away, but she felt the need to explain the best she could. How different the times were, how helpless and ashamed she felt.

He placed his hand over hers, assuring her he had wonderful parents who loved him, and her choice led him to meeting Terry, whose picture he showed her on his i phone.
His utter delight with his wife was apparent, as he fumbled to find the best photos of her.

Throughout dinner, Charlotte was struck by his confidence, his poise in dealing with the staff at De Marco's, many of whom he knew. How easily he had chatted with the crew from The Beacon. Her small package had been cared for by good people, and she felt all traces of jealousy and resentment fade away. They made a plan for her to meet Terry and his dad later that week.

While walking her to her cab, more boyish and less poised, he said, "Watch the fireworks with us this year." And with his eyes glancing sideways, he whispered, "I always hoped for that."

"I did too, son. Every.... Single.... Day."

Charlotte asked the cab driver to take her to The Beacon. Frankie promised they'd find a way to keep the place open for her, no matter what. And they did.

From: Potluck Magazine

SURFING ON MY LEFT FOOT

It was shortly after the divorce when I met Jody. She was serving
punch at a party for the newly - single. My sons told me about the
party which jolted me. I prided myself on my devotion to them,
watching my language, dressing conservatively, and cutting off the
perils of romance. They probably knew I was lonely.

"Try some. It's got a nice bite to it," Jody said, pointing to
the chilled pink bowl. She was friendly, direct, and had a great
laugh. " I have to drive," I said, and she let me know it was a soft
drink. " The bite is just grenadine."... I needed a second opinion.
The driving part was true, but I had to be sure. Already needing to
please Jody, I made sure she wasn't looking as I asked another
woman about the punch. "It's in the by-laws. Punch is soft. Alcohol
out on the sun porch."

I enjoyed her droll response, later learning that it was nearly
true. The group had been sued and needed full disclosure vis-à-vis
alcohol. I walked back over to the punch bowl and Jody. " How did
you get this job?" I asked her feeling brave.

" Punch bowl supervisor? Nobody else wanted it," she said,
and I reached out my hand to shake hers. "Michelle McGee. Nice
to meet you."

"Jody Cooper." She moved from behind the table when she
shook my hand. I felt welcomed, yet shy.

She deftly pulled me toward a group near us saying, "Meet
Michelle McGee. I just did."

I noticed how well-liked she seemed to be by the small group leaning against the mantle. The party was in an old beach cottage and some of it's features reminded me of my grandparent's house in Philly. The mantle especially, with the circular wooden grapes painted white on its surface.

Each of them gave me his name. Most were charming, and a few of the guys were attractive. The avalanche of parenthood was a shared feature among this group. Few things were worse on a date, than a neat guy's surprise about your kids.

I noticed an attractive couple and wondered why they chose this gathering. He pushed a strand of her sandy hair behind her ear. She blushed and saw me checking them out. She walked away from him toward me and introduced herself.

"I'm Amy Brewer. My husband Richard does business for the group."

In the course of the conversation, she told me she owned the gift shop on Meade Street.

"The Cup and Saucer?" I said, trying not to giggle.

"I inherited the name. What can I tell you?" she said warmly. "The tourists love it, especially the older ones. 'I'm sick of mugs' I've heard mumbled more than a few times. "

Although the window display showed delicate dish sets, the store sold nearly anything a tourist family might need. And plenty of mugs. My son found a worn baseball glove there. We weren't tourists per se, but my sons and I were new to this part of the sea shore town.

After Tom's decision to end our marriage, we sold our home and the boys and I moved a few blocks closer to the ocean. They were both avid surfers, and I loved the sea. Our rental could practically fit into the garage of our old house, but we all needed the change.

They didn't have to switch schools which was a major consideration. For all of us.

Jody guided me to the sun porch, pointing to the little step down to enter. The windows were open and I could smell the ocean. And the booze.

"How bout I fix you something a little stronger?" she said.

"I don't drink."

While fixing herself a vodka tonic, she asked me about my kids.

She understood my simple response about drinking, and didn't push things further.

I liked her. And told her about my sons.

Her children were girls and we shared i phone photos. There had been a divorce. We spared one another the details, as we had been christened on a similar journey. More like bludgeoned, but we liked each other for leaving that unsaid.

"Did you meet Amy Brewer?" Jody asked me as we both stepped outside to breathe in the salt air.

"I just did. She told me about her shop."

"Amy is my boss." Jody said. "Part time. My girls don't push, but with i-phones, clothes and stuff, it adds up."

"And surf boards," I added.

"Her husband Richard's law firm handled a few things for the group. She and Richard were probably dropping off paperwork to the chairman," Jody said.

We exchanged contact information and I left the party with a slight smile.

My son Thomas broke from his tai chi to ask me how the party was.

My heart contracted for him...For us.

"I met a friend," I said, pleased with his attention.

"A guy friend?" he said with a wary look.

Good. I thought. My boys aren't ready for that either.

"No. A woman named Jody. She organizes these parties and works at "The Cup and Saucer. "

"Where Sean got his glove," he said returning to his form.

"Mom. It's all in the balance. The big waves have no mercy," he said looking like Bruce Lee. I was glad he was back to himself and no longer worried about me.

The next day I kept checking my cell for a message from Jody, feeling like a high school girl. I decided to be the grown-up and contact her first.

And then, I chickened out.

She sent me a text just when I pulled back, seeming to sense my absurd shyness.

"Great meeting you, Michelle. Coffee sometime?"

So she truly got the message of my sobriety. Coffee. Then my mind started whirling into one of its orbits. Without the divorce, I wouldn't have met her. Without the drinking, I may still be married. Without sobriety, I would be insane or dead.

My son Sean opened the fridge behind me and I realized I needed to text her back.

'   "Tuesday night work for you?"

There. I did it. Combined a sprinkle of assertiveness training with sales tactics I picked up in a summer sales job.

Starbucks had made its way to our coastal New Jersey town, and it was there that I met Jody to launch a friendship. As many women do, we covered a lot of ground about our early life, families, likes and dislikes. Although we were both parents, each of us faced different challenges, she mothering girls, and I raising boys. We both were slightly wistful that we wouldn't know the experience of rearing both genders.

"They say boys are easier,' she offered.

"And girls stay close." I replied.

" But what do they know?" We both blurted out simultaneously.

Before we finished, she told me Amy was looking for help at her shop for the busy summer season. Jody already knew I was a teacher and would be free this summer, and we were open about our expenses.

The next day after school, I walked the few short blocks to Meade Street to talk to Amy. I was proud of my newfound spunkiness, emerging from a lifetime of timid restraint. My ex was punctual with the child support, but money was a strain since the divorce.

As I entered The Cup and Saucer, I was greeted with the scent of lavender. Amy remembered my name.

" Michelle McGee. You found us."

Right on the spot, I was happy we had moved. People were friendly and open. I missed my beautiful home farther from the coast, but not the stuffiness of many of my neighbors. It seemed as if the ocean worked its magic on the people close to it.

"May I help you find anything in this mess of a place? " Amy said, obviously proud of her shop.

Feeling my shyness return, I smiled and asked to look around.

I took a few deep yoga-type breaths, reminding myself to get back to regular practice.
The shop was far from a mess. Things followed a logical order with beach toys and clothes being the most prominent. Most of the food was in the same section, close to the toiletries that so many vacationers forget to pack. Amy didn't hover or make me feel uncomfortable, so I repeated a yoga breath, walked up to her and asked for a job.

She giggled and said. "Relax. I don't bite."

She did give off the confidence of a person who had never clipped a coupon or drank store brand soda.

We went back and forth about how many hours I wanted, her biggest rush times, and she hired me with a hand shake. I almost forgot to give Jody the footnote, as I thought of the word reference, after years of teaching.

"Jody Cooper encouraged me to ask you. Thank you both," I said, after we had exchanged contact information. I nearly skipped home as my luck felt as if it were changing for the good.

I took a week off between the end of the school year and beginning my work at the gift shop. Jody, though not a teacher, worked in the school district too. Neither of us was free for full time work and Amy trusted us to juggle our hours without involving her. Amy posted the schedule on a cork board outside her office and the part-timers penciled in changes as things came up. It worked out well.

Almost immediately, Jody and I found ways to make our schedules coincide. We were developing a friendship, enjoying one another's humor, and loosening up Amy. When we were sure the shop had no visitors, we tossed a small rubber baseball and threw a plastic basketball into a net. They teased me that I could only throw with my right hand. They were far more ambidextrous than I.

Jody, the most athletic of the three of us, sometimes stepped outside to jump and touch the Cup and Saucer sign as so many young men did to signs and awnings in town.

Sometimes I would notice Amy squaring her shoulders and pursing her lips to remind herself that she was the owner and shouldn't be treating her shop like a playground.
I pointed this out to Jody.

"Oh, please, Michelle," she said one day as we walked along the ocean after our shift. "Richard makes a ton of money. Don't worry about Amy's boutique."

I winced at the comment finding it belittling and sarcastic. My balloon of euphoria was pricked with unease about Jody. I didn't feel that our failed marriages had any relationship to Amy's thriving one.

In her charismatic way, Jody diminished my doubts about her by inviting me to join them for the six o'clock yoga class. Knowing that Amy was more of a friend than boss to Jody made me feel better about Jody's remarks.

I left a note for my sons with instructions to re-heat the lasagna. Each could program any techie device in the land with the exception of the microwave. Battling my shyness, I grabbed my yoga mat and drove to the studio.

Both Jody and Amy had already set up their mats, towels and water jugs.

When the teacher walked in I went into child's pose hoping she didn't notice me.
I knew her from other studios, which is so often the case with yoga instructors. She had an
annoying habit of calling me out on my weak left side.

"Michelle, you must trust your left side, your left foot."

During this class, I was spared a public call-out by the teacher, but she did whisper to me during tree pose on our left foot. "Work on the left side balance, dear."

After class Amy said, "Join us for a beer at Langan's."
Jody's eyes widened and I knew she hadn't said anything to Amy about my recovery. The Jody likeability meter hit a gong over the top.

Not only was Amy incapable of guile, Jody had respected my privacy.

Wow. I was making friends.

"My boys are home alone, but you two have fun," I said, as I practically skipped to my car, mat rolled under my arm like the cool yogis do.

During my third week of work, the Jody meter took a dive when I saw her pocket a twenty that a tourist gave her. I was coming around the corner and I saw she didn't ring in the beach towel the guy bought.

"That'll be $19.50" she said in her winning way while handing the customer fifty cents change from her pocket. She slid the twenty into her other pocket.

And then I saw her do it with a couple of ten dollar bills.

My reaction to this was extreme. I chose not to share it at my next meeting and then found excuses to avoid meetings altogether. I found myself walking by Mahoney's Liquor, eyeing a bottle of Jack Daniels.

Deep in my gut, I knew I had not grieved the death of my marriage and expected my new friends to prove to me that life was still fun, that I was worthwhile. In my zeal to protect my sons, and avoid being another divorcée with a sob story, I had hampered my growth and thrown my expectations on my new friend Jody.

This had to stop. I had work to do. I had to scream, wail, throw a few glasses at a wall somewhere. Maybe I would blow up a pic of my ex's face and throw darts at it. I would find the privacy when the boys were with their dad.

I told Jody when we were alone in the shop, what I had seen. She gave me the rant about Amy's rich husband, and I told her I may tell Amy. I couldn't believe the courage it took me to stand up to her. Whether or not I told Amy became less important to me than facing my fears, my need to be liked, my life in recovery from the bottle and from losing the man I loved.

I nearly sprinted to a meeting that very evening saying little but preparing myself for some changes in my life.

Maybe after the dart board episode, when my body was limp from crying, I would begin the climb out of the dark hole of grief. Maybe I would grab one of my boys' surf boards and take the damned thing into the ocean and learn to surf, to balance and sway, my body having felt the pain of loss. I was going to fall and get back up, to feel strength on my left side, healing in my heart, to balance and surf on my left foot.

From: The Eleventh Transmission

GAM

Grandmother let me set the table. Billy pulled out the leaf to make it bigger when there were lots of people. "We will use the linens for the guests- our best tablecloth, Ellen."

I enjoyed polishing the silver with the bluish cream and the soft blue cloth. She set up my work shop on the porch at a table covered with newspaper. This way I could smell the ocean, hear the seagulls squawking, and watch the boats going by. I counted the boats, forgetting to work.

"She's dreamy, Esther," I could hear her telling her sister in whispered tones on the black phone in the kitchen. I could imagine great aunt Esther saying something creepy about me. Mommy used to turn up her shoulder when Aunt Esther came to town. She had the same look when we ran into Mr. Wicker, her boss at the bank, when we met him at the grocery store . "Mr. Wicked" was her name for him. She said that to her friends in her quiet voice.

I remember only pieces of the day it happened. My neighbor Sarah, in the middle of balloons the scary clown was shaping into animals. I snuck an extra piece of cake when nobody was looking, as sugary treats were new to me. When I saw the policeman talking to Sarah's Mom, I thought I was in trouble for my theft. His big hand felt like sandpaper as he guided me to the fancy living room where no kids were playing. Sarah's Mom stood behind the purple chair, it's edge too plump for her fingers.

I do remember my grandmother coming to Sarah's to get me. Policemen held on to her and the clown bumped into her. "Accident. Hospital. Heaven."

I think I heard those words, or maybe learned them in the meetings I had with the nice lady who lived near grandmother. In the year since it happened, I saw the lady a lot. "Ellen" she would say to me, when I couldn't look at her, "Tell me how you feel." I loved Gam so much, I was afraid to tell the lady how sad I was. How much I missed Mommy.

The day my grandmother agreed to a nickname was sunny. We had come to the porch to play cards and watch the ocean. "Gam. I want to call you Gam," I said, looking at the ocean. She pulled back her lower lip and said. "Ellen, Gam it shall be!"

Gam turned little things into a celebration.

"How many flowers are on that tree?"

"Who cares if the recipe says cinnamon? No need sending Billy out for that."

Billy lived next door. One of the Gilligans. They had a lot of kids. He went to a special school. Gam paid him for the chores she needed done since Grandpa died. Gam's voice changed when Billy was around. She left spaces like Reverend Miller did after his stroke.

Gam and I brought dinners to the Millers. She would leave them on their doorstep. She let me clang the hanging bell on the door as a signal. Even though Gam was sad Reverend had to retire, she still played word games with me on the sandy road to their cottage.

"Let's pick new names for everything we see, Ellen."

"The gifts of sight and speech....And your imagination. Use them! Enjoy them!"

Miss Dixon didn't like Gam's games. She called Gam into school to meet with her.
I wasn't allowed to go, but I knew it wouldn't be fun. Miss Dixon didn't like fun. Or me.

"Esther, she wants her to color between the lines," Gam said, not bothering to whisper.

I was kind of confused because I was good at coloring. Even Miss Dixon said so.

Then Gam started whispering again. I tip-toed through the hall, careful not to step on the noisy floor board.

"Not one word of sympathy about my Julia. Nothing." Gam got quiet. I think she was crying. Julia was Mommy. Oh how I missed Mommy! I stood still as a statue. Mommy used to be little like me. It was hard to picture Mommy jumping rope or coloring.

I wanted to ask Gam all about Mommy, but I didn't want to make her cry, like Miss Dixon did. But Miss Dixon didn't ask about Mommy. I knew that made Gam sad. Everything about Mommy made us sad.

The next day I asked Miss Dixon if she liked my coloring.

"It's good, Ellen. But we're doing subtraction now."

When we got to poetry, Miss Dixon told me to sit down and study it better. I had said sparrow for bird and violet for purple. I remembered that Miss Dixon wasn't Gam.

That evening Gam and I played cards on the porch. The waves were big and loud, and the birds were squealing like crazy. Gam lifted her tea cup and smiled at me."I dropped off the peach pie we made to the Reverend today. Mrs. Miller told me she didn't feel up to planning a birthday party for him. I'd said we'd do it, Ellen."

Just then, a big white bird landed on the porch railing. It was as big as me, and had a pink tail. "Our first guest, Ellen! A spoonbill!"

After Gam read me a bedtime story, I crept over to my encyclopedia, to look up spoonbill. It wasn't a made-up name. There was a pretty picture of it. I needed to get things straight for Miss Dixon.

Gam walked me to the Millers more than usual, to ask about the party.

One windy day, we passed Danny Gilligan, Billy's older brother, opening the car door for his mother, just like the movies. He wore bright red sneakers that came up to his ankles. They had a white star near the top.

"I wish I could drive a car. When I get bigger, I will."

"Don't wish your life away, Ellen. There is a time for everything."

"No....church....people, " Reverend said to us. Mrs. Miller's face got red like mine when Miss Dixon corrected me. "He doesn't want to exclude anyone. Or make you work too hard," she said to Gam.

"Then we'll have a small luncheon. We'll invite the Gilligans and my sister, Esther."

Oh no, I thought. Aunt Esther could ruin anything. Later that evening, I was happy to hear Aunt Esther couldn't make it. Then I felt bad because she was Gam's sister. And Mommy's aunt.

The day of the party was sunny and bright. Billy came over early to pull out the leaf to make the table big enough. Gam and I put on a light brown table cloth with pretty yellow flowers. I folded the linen napkins and placed the silverware I polished where Gam had taught me.

Billy opened the windows. He had put in the screens earlier that week.

Gam and I baked a big square birthday cake for Reverend Miller.

The Gilligan family were our first guests. I was disappointed that Danny couldn't come. His Mom said he had to work. Danny was nice to little kids. Billy told me Danny's job was with kids, when he wasn't in school.

Mrs. Miller pushed her husband's wheel chair up to the table. She asked Gam to sit down and relax. "You've done enough. Sit down and enjoy this fine food," she said.

We said grace and began to eat. There was a knock on the front door. Billy answered it.

I noticed Danny's sneakers as he walked into the room. He had a big red bulb on his nose, and a costume like a clown. I thought of the clown the day Mommy died, but remembered it was Danny. He said hello to everyone and waved his squirt bottle.

Gam screamed and pushed away from the table. She let out a sob so loud, it nearly broke my heart. Her shoulders shook as she put her hands to her face. "Julia," she said through her hiccups.

Mrs. Gilligan led her family from the table. Mrs. Miller put her arms around Gam.

"I'll read you a story, Gam. I'll make you tea," I said.

Mrs. Miller looked over at me, and I knew it was time to be quiet. I listened to the noisy seagulls outside. I made up stories that they told each other. Stories I would tell grandmother later, when her shoulders stopped shaking.

I could picture Gam in her porch chair smiling, drinking tea, sitting up straight and still.....still, like the spoonbill who visited us before the party.

From: Potluck Magazine

THE BOARDING HOUSE

Mr. Maguire the boarder parked in the same spot every day. But that wasn't what made him strange. I had plenty of time to watch him when my older brother dropped me for girls and baseball. I noticed Mr. Maguire's quirky ways, like walking on a slant with his newspaper over his head even on sunny days.

The boarding house butted up against the back yard of the house we lived in when we were little. My parents hadn't been able to afford the dream house they were always talking about.

After a day of packing boxes at the plant, my father would say to my mother, "Bernadette, we'll have a yard big enough for a tractor-mower, and a basketball net for Denny in the driveway."

My mother, saint that she was, would listen to his dreams, wide-eyed and smiling, as if she never heard them before.

"And you'll look so handsome, Charlie, riding your mower."

I didn't understand how she could keep it up, day after day. We were broke. Our house was a dump, and my entertainment was watching the weirdos in the boarding house out back. Especially, Mr. Maguire.

My boring life became more exciting when I noticed one day that Mr. Maguire switched parking spots. At first I thought it was a mirage, as I squinted from the morning sun. The crack in our dirty window didn't help. But there was his rust-colored Buick pulling into a spot close to the residents' entrance. His gait was swift as he rounded the driver's side to the trunk. He opened it and gently lifted out an oblong case with the care of a mother lifting her baby.

He held the case close to his chest and straightened up, looking less slanted.

I wonder what is making Mr. Maguire so transfixed? I probably didn't know that word at the time, but the memory of his transformation is imprinted in my mind, and that's the word I'm thinking now, years after our ascent into the suburbs.

He closed the trunk gently and he advanced toward the boarding house, moving the case to his left arm as he opened the door for Miss Perkins to come out. She was probably en route to the bus stop. I knew her routine too.

My interest in the residents was escalating into an obsession.

"Bernadette, Teresa spends too much time at that window," my father whispered, on a rare day off from work.

"She's dreamy like you, Charlie."

I knew it wouldn't be long before I crept over to the boarding house to see what was what. No matter what I saw, I wouldn't tell my brother who had the biggest mouth on the block.

Mr. Maguire, whom I was beginning to consider my friend, made things easier for me when he exited the door visible from my perch at the grimy window. He held his thin body more upright now as he carried the case clutched to his chest.

Grateful that I was fully dressed to go out, and that I had already promised to go to the grocery store, I called "Bye, Mom" before she could think up an excuse to keep me home. My mother may have painted rainbows with my Dad, but she was, at heart, a stark realist who knew the dangers of the city.

I followed Mr. Maguire down the street, checking my grocery list so I could whip through Caruso's Market quickly. My mother might have had a stop watch. She knew down to the minute how long an errand should last.

I had gotten to know the tilt of the boarder's gait so well, that I could see the difference in him these days. He walked nearly upright to the little park on the corner. When he reached a bench, he opened the case and pulled out a violin. He sat gazing tenderly at the caramel-colored instrument. Two harmless-looking older women chose seats on a bench near him. A look of panic overtook him. I was behind a tree and could see perfectly.

Did it take courage to come out of hiding to speak to him?

Perhaps. Especially since a side-trip to the park would show up on my mother's stop watch. I walked over to him and said, "Do you know how to play it?"

He nodded. And he began to play a tune that haunts me till today. "The Tennessee Waltz."

When he sang aloud the line *I remember the night and the Tennessee Waltz*, a tear fell down his cheek. I figured Mrs. Maguire was 'a bad sort' as my grandmother was fond of saying. The ladies on the bench were as quiet as if in church at dawn. Mr. Maguire nodded to them when he finished.

"And you are?" he said to me.

"Teresa McMahon...after the saint...You know, St. Teresa and all that."

I had the sense to stop talking. I thought of my father saying it was good to be still and quiet sometimes.

"Thank you, Teresa."

That was the beginning of an opening in me.

"Thank you, Teresa."

I rolled the words around in my head, dying to tell my mother or brother.

Somebody thanked me for something. He didn't say, "Wear your boots" or "Help me with groceries." He said, "Thank you."

I sprung into a sprint to Caruso's Market with my list a tattered mess from balling my fists in my pockets. Ketchup, mustard, paper napkins.

"They'll be linen napkins in the new house, Charlie."

"Bernadette, we can have them now. I'll work overtime to get them."

"Charlie, you work too much. I've got my stash. If I wanted linen napkins, we'd have them."

I could recite their loving words to every shrink I saw after my brother Denny was struck by a bus on his way home from baseball, never to be with us again.

I could re-create my mother's shrieks and wails from Denny's room, not one item moved or changed. And how animated Denny became when he made the All-Star team. The panic that rocked me in a plush doctor's office when I started to forget the features of his face, the sound of his voice. The funds my parents received from the transport company took us places that had only been jokes among us, our ability to laugh now stunted by my brother's absence.

My mother's faith was tested, her wooden rosary worn down to a nub.

In a rare fit of rage, my father threw the rosary against the kitchen wall, a wall the color of mustard.

"Don't blaspheme the Lord, Charlie. Teresa is here," she whispered through a strangled sob.

"I thought she was at that damned boarding house," my father said.

Through the crushing pain of loss, I clung to Mr. Maguire as a source of strength. I learned there had been no Mrs. Maguire, only the hope for one, but she had been lost to another suitor, as in the lyrics of "The Tennessee Waltz".

He let me cry about Denny during the concerts he began performing at the boarding house. I tried to be strong for my parents as we crawled through the days without Denny, an inch at a time. Mr. Maguire also didn't give me religious mumbo jumbo like my Mom did. He just let me be sad.

Miss Perkins was fond of the music that flowed from Mr. Maguire's violin. We, too, formed a friendship of sorts, much of it unspoken. She squeezed my hand, her fingers nubby with arthritis. And when the residents scattered after the musical performance, she would remain with Mr. Maguire and me.

"I told my parents your music is beautiful, Mr. Maguire."

"Thank you, Teresa."

On a hot July afternoon, my mother invited Mr. Maguire over for iced tea. She asked him to bring his violin to play "Amazing Grace" in Denny's room. All of us wept openly. When my father walked him back to the boarding house, my elderly friend stood tall, his gifts to us somehow releasing him as well.

Years later, long after Mr. Maguire was playing his violin in Heaven, my mother called me from their lovely home in the suburbs to tell me the boarding house was being demolished.

During dinner with my parents for my thirtieth birthday, Charlie was still painting rainbows and Bernadette was enhancing each one with her love.

From: Spadina Magazine

MAKING FRIENDS

Smitty left his flask on the street when they picked him up. Guess he didn't want to make things worse. But the cops were nice. Something about a daughter at the station. I pictured the hot burn in my throat, but didn't drink any. Gave it to Lester when he set his box near mine in Smitty's old spot.

From: Blink Ink

THE PERILS OF MOVING DAY

Kevin's friend Roger backed his truck into my driveway. I could
hear the swoosh of the mattress going through the door. I was in
the kitchen, not trusting the guys with my grandmother's china. I
had lined the boxes with newspaper, and chosen white tissue paper
to surround each delicate piece.

I heard the screen door shut, and inhaled the scent of azalea
bushes surrounding the entrance to my place. So, it was decided.
Kevin and I were moving in together. My parents wouldn't
approve, so I hadn't told them.

"Katie," Kevin would say, as he put down the remote to look
at me.

"Why pay for two places, and run back and forth forgetting
half our stuff?"

"Kevin, that was the least romantic proposal I've ever heard," I
said, grateful for our easy ways, but sometimes I wanted more
tradition between us.

Like an engagement ring sitting poised on a delicate gold
band, presented to me in a small blue box. Stories my aunts liked
to tell during card games my mother held when I was little.
Remembering all the romance before my uncles, those still among
us, sprouted beer bellies, and were taken over by their remote
controls, switching one loud game for another.

From my vantage point, there was no dimming of the love my
aunts and uncles shared, stretched and grown through the turmoil
of children and layoffs. Their girl talk, unguarded with my

mother's blush wine, proudly served in stemmed glasses, let them reminisce their dreams when love was new; their waists tiny; and their hopes untainted with age or loss.

Was I craving these traditions my aunts spoke of so colorfully, or was something off between Kevin and me? I could list the friends and family who spoke of my luck in having met him and sparked his interest. I was in complete agreement to the point of feeling defensive of my own worthiness, and few things were as captivating as Kevin's eyes...when he removed himself from the sports viewing that so consumed his free time.

And then there was the trickle of doubt that swept through me when I thought of Richard and the charge between us that rocked my world. His saying he needed space, and wasn't ready for commitment; my wobbly re entry into the world of dating; the smoky-eyed guy who applied ice to my head when I slipped at a party wearing too high heels - the guy I was moving in with today.

"Katie," he said, peeking into the kitchen. I nearly dropped my grandma's gravy dish. "We need you to go to Home Depot to get more packing boxes. Roger's buddies will be here in two hours."

Typical Kevin to let things go to the last minute. Home Depot was the last place I wanted to be on a Saturday. I shifted gears, got a better head about it, and went to my car, squeezed in at the corner.

Given to believing in celestial signs and signals, I breathed a sigh of relief when I found a parking spot close to the entrance of the store. Perhaps this move was blessed by the gods. As I asked an orange- aproned employee to direct me to the boxes, I caught sight of a profile that ground me to a halt. I hid behind a sign to take a better look.

The old familiar jolt, the high that was everything Richard hit me like a shot of Jack   Daniels. I missed that spark, but not the slights, the freeze-outs....the angst.

He spotted me, placed the tools he was holding onto a display table, and gifted me with one of his heart-stopping smiles. I stayed put and he came over and pulled me close to him. I remembered

his scent and the turmoil of his infidelities, and my leaning on
Aunt Sally during one of our episodes.

"He's not the right one, Katie. You'll know it when you meet
him. My parents hated Tony at first, but I knew...and he never
disappointed me, 'did you Tony?' "she said to the empty placemat.
"All that glitters isn't gold" she added, my tears welling up
again, loving her, and missing Uncle Tony.

"Katie, it's so good to see you," Richard said, bringing me
back to the present.
'Catch a coffee?" He said confidently.
He had the look he had when I made him fess up that he did
hit on my friend Mariah.

"No thanks, Richard," I said, "Give my best to your parents,"
I said, meaning it.
I didn't check out any boxes, and felt in my bones that Kevin
was not right for me. I turned and headed to my car knowing that
we wouldn't be moving in together, not today...not ever. His
kindness had healed me from the dregs of my break-up with
Richard, but he didn't inflame me as Richard had, and I knew there
was somebody out there who could make me feel what Aunt Sally
felt for Uncle Tony, somebody with Kevin's goodness who sparked
me as had Richard, without his glaring flaws.

It wouldn't be easy disappointing Kevin, but he deserved
better than what I felt for him.

The sound of Aunt Sally's voice on the phone overwhelmed
me with relief. She accepted my dropping by for a quick chat, to
shore me up for what I was facing, and would not disappoint me in
her counsel or her kindness.

From: The Phoenix Issue

104

AFTERNOONS WITH THE ROGANS

Aunt Kate used to pick me up in her black Dodge. My mother treated me to ribbons in my hair on the days Aunt Kate worked there.

"They're lace curtain," Momma would say, an expression that sprinkled my youth with visions of opulence and splendor. "'Tis how they can afford Kate's fussing with hems and gowns."

I tried not to let Momma see how happy I was to spend an afternoon with the Rogans.

From the moment Mrs. Rogan opened the door, I felt I donned the cape of a royal person. Sweet smells emanated from the big kitchen, and during the spring and summer, the scent of freshly cut grass added to my sense of comfort.

Mr. Rogan probably never threw a beer bottle across a room in his life. Mrs. Rogan called him "my Jim" when she spoke to Aunt Kate, but to me and the neighborhood kids, it was "Mr. Rogan."

The neighborhood kids were not playing stickball or dodge ball in the street. They were swimming in one of the backyard pools, or sunning themselves in lounge chairs like grown-ups. Mrs. Rogan often encouraged me to bring my swim suit and join the family across the street. Fearful, at first, I resisted the invitation. But one day, I ventured across the street and one of the Martins said, " Get your suit. We're playing Marco Polo." That sealed it for me. The next time Aunt Kate treated me to an afternoon with the Rogans, I was going to be ready to swim with the Martins.

But I wasn't going to let Momma know. Not wanting to feel less than the Rogans and their "fancy neighbors," Momma would have felt sad for me, not having those kinds of things, and sad for herself, for Poppa's inability to provide them. And I would do anything to avoid making Momma sad. Just about anything, but when the turquoise water rolled over me, or one of the Martins invited me for water volleyball, Momma was of no concern to me whatsoever.

One afternoon, Aunt Kate nearly hissed at me, "Maggie, Mrs. Rogan asked you a question," tilting her head toward her boss.

"She's dreamy, Kate. Not to worry about my foolish questions," Mrs. Rogan said without an ounce of guile. I was so taken with the arrangement of tulips and daffodils and the bees visiting them, I didn't hear Mrs. Rogan speak to me.

"Your garden is beautiful," I said, surprising myself with my assertion. The Martin kids and their friends were rubbing off on me, and Momma could smell it. I could tell by the arch of her eyebrow, when I glared at Daddy during one of his rages.

"Why thank you, Maggie. The Mr. Loves doing it, but rarely has time. I schedule the gardeners when he isn't here," she whispered gently. And then she got a faraway look as if she knew this was all temporary, a fact I was clearly not ready to accept. I also got the feeling she brought in her sister and their daughters to give my Aunt Kate work.

Mrs. Rogan's niece, Ellen, was clearly not interested in the finery Aunt Kate stitched for her, but seemed to have inherited her aunt's grace in keeping that from Aunt Kate, who would have been mortified if she thought Mrs. Rogan was making work for her. Her "Dodge was bought and paid for with her own bare hands." It was oft heard phrase that still makes me smile and miss my Aunt Kate.

Aunt Kate and the Rogans couldn't have known how much they influenced my decision to live a genteel life, where glowing with affection for one's spouse and children was completely acceptable, desirable behavior.

I met Grant at the U of P where my grades and SAT scores opened the doors of the Ivy League whose students reminded me more of the Brogans than my own family. Some bell rang in me that this man was familiar to me as if we knew each other in a past life or something. Beneath the instant spark of attraction was a sense of safety and endurance I felt in him.

He called when he said he would, which deviated from my experience with guys who complicated my life with unkindness. Initially, I was slightly repelled by Grant's directness, of his not needing to hit on my friends, or notice my extra five pounds. He liked me and respected my time. I loved him after I cured myself of my inability to accept his unpolluted interest in me.

Without my afternoons with the Rogans, I would never have met Grant and felt worthy of his interest. Nor do I think Poppa would have found the group whose friends treated him so much better than any of his bar room buddies, and put the spark back in Momma's eyes.

When my behavior at home became more assertive and yet more cordial, something seeped into the wallpaper of the O'Neill home. My parents reached for a second chance in life, and as I sit here waiting for my grandson, Grant the fourth or fifth, I rejoice that my Aunt Kate was spunky enough to carve a path out of the way things were, into the way things could be.

Although I never referred to my late husband as "my Grant," I did alight at the turn of his key after a day of work, and greet him with all the joy and affection of Mrs. Rogan for her Jim.

From: Scarlet Leaf Review

MEETING MELISSA

The gate guard's voice was different. Less deferential.

"Mrs. Palmer, there's a young woman named Melissa here to see you. "

"Did she tell you her last name? I don't know a Melissa, nor am I expecting one, Officer Williams."

" She said she worked in Mr. Palmer's Chicago office." Jack…. The gate guard mentioned Jack as if he were still alive. As if all were not lost to me.

"Doris," I said, breaking the protocol of Sailfish Cove, with its Officer this and Mrs. That. "Does she seem dangerous?"

"Not for me to say, Mrs. Palmer," she said, "but she seems O.K. And, of course I had a good look at her license."

"Please send her in, Officer Williams. And enjoy your evening," I said, and she added, "I should have said something earlier. I'm so sorry, Mrs. Palmer. The Mr. was never too busy to greet me and the other guards, and we appreciated it."

Jack wouldn't notice differences in people's occupational status, as driven and ambitious as he was in his work. He endeared himself to everyone he met. Maybe a bit too much to attractive women, but even then, he was guileless and remained, in his mind, the geek who couldn't woo the girl. But woo me he did, enough for me to be admitting a stranger who said she knew him in his Chicago office,

Trusting the guard's instincts, I prepared myself to meet someone who knew my Jack. As her silver Honda pulled into my driveway, I had a moment of panic that she had come to harm me, but enduring the chronic grief was so debilitating, I didn't care what she did to me.

Or so I thought.

"Mrs. Palmer, I'm Melissa Hobart, and I knew Mr. Palmer from the Slater office in Chicago."

Keeping the door slightly open, I summoned my most formal Sailfish Cove tone, and said, "What may I do for you, Ms. Hobart?"

She fumbled in her purse and I feared a gun, and nearly slammed the door. Her slender fingers produced an i-phone photo from Slater with Jack surrounded by employees, including her.

"Come on in Melissa," I said and directed her to the den.

"Would you like coffee, water…a soda?"

"No, I'm good, Mrs. Palmer."

"Call me Kathy," I said as I went into the kitchen and grabbed two bottles of water, relieved that I feared the imagined gun. Perhaps my depression was a sliver lessened.

I sat across from Melissa in one of our matching eggshell colored couches, and I noticed she devoured the water, after thanking me.

"I wanted to meet you. " she said directly, and then rolled her tongue over her upper lip and said, "Mr. Palmer told me about you."

Oh no, I thought, Jack was not only unfaithful, he had dipped into the twenty year old set.

"You knew Mr. Palmer well enough to discuss me?" I said fearfully.

"Whatever went on between the two of you…." I trailed off, kicking myself for how wimpy I sounded. Why couldn't I behave like the heroines of stage and screen who delivered the perfect line with grit and panache?

Melissa looked over at the painting on the wall, and there was something in her profile that was vaguely familiar. I had a few cousins in Chicago whom I never met.

"Are we related ?" I blurted out.

"Sort of," she said, as she repeated that tongue rolling thing, and I knew. She was related to Jack. By blood.

"He said he was going to tell you, or I would have done this differently."

"Tell me what?"

She opened her mouth, then closed it, and after a few seconds said,

"That I'm his daughter."

I got up from the couch and paced around the kitchen trying to do the math. She seemed about twenty. That would have put us smack in the middle of Manhattan and the fertility specialist.

I grabbed the edge of the kitchen entry and said slowly and maliciously, "How old are you?"

"I turned nineteen in May," she said earnestly.

In the way shock lets normal thoughts through, I thought how open young people are.

Here comes this little creep to ruin my life, and she has no clenched fists or shoulders. No fear that I may be extremely fond of my Second Amendment rights. She just sat there, living proof of my failure to give birth, with a guileless, open expression.

"I'm a Taurus," she said, as if that explained everything.

I sat down on the couch across from her and surprised myself by saying, "When I lost Jack, I didn't want to go on living."

She started to speak, but then looked at me instead.

"Waking up, thinking he was at work, and remembering the horror of it all. Or watching one of our crime shows, and turning to tell him who was the villain, and seeing his spot on the couch empty. Nothing you have to say to me can be worse than that, or at least that's what I thought until now."

"Mrs. Palmer, I thought you knew. My mother thought you did."

Her mother. There was no way I was ready to hear any details about Jack's other woman. Clearly, the man and the marriage I was mourning were a sham. I didn't want to cry in front of Melissa, and I needed time to absorb the shock of infidelity. Maybe there were countless other women and maybe other children, which pierced me, and reminded me of the torture of trying to conceive.

Feeling as if Melissa meant me no harm, I fumbled for my i-phone and asked her to enter her contact information.

"Please leave, "I said, as I made my way to the front door and held it open.

She didn't say anything, but I noticed her eyes were watery and she did the lip thing...so like Jack. As devastated as I was by his deception, I had a sense that I would need to meet with Melissa again. There was so much I needed to know.

I went to the fridge and popped open a soda, and returned to the couch...the spot where I heard the news that exploded my universe. Jack loved another woman, and I never sensed it. My mind went through the time nine months before the May Melissa was born. Blessed or cursed with a photographic memory of dates and time. I could re-create my birthday in July that year, and the frequent trips to New York to the doctor who promised us a baby. I had no clear memory of Chicago trips during that time, but did remember several hurricane warnings that kept Jack from flying home.

As I sipped my Pepsi, I mentally repeated Jack's many assurances that I was enough for him with or without a child. That we were enough. That we were a complete circle unto ourselves. What a crock, I thought as the tears started to flow. My silent critics during the services who thought me heartless and stoic would be pleased to see my tears, to see me behave like a normal widow...whatever that was.

More than ever, I wished I had a sister to comfort me. I envied the tales of sisterly support and fun from the time I was a small child, talking to my dolls, pretending they were the siblings I didn't have. I couldn't share these feelings with my Mom as she'd hoped for a house full of kids, and was only able to have me, Kathy Dolan, the only child surrounded by all the Mc Gee and Conway kids.

And when one of the Conway kids envied my mounds of Christmas presents, I envied the squeals of delight and banter in their home.

In spite of the living proof of Jack's secret life, I consoled myself that he did love me and my desire for a child interfered with our closeness.....until we gave up. We had ruled out adoption for various reasons, and as I pedaled backward in time, the year before Melissa's birth was not one of our good ones.

However, the taste of betrayal was very bitter. I got up and poured my soda down the sink and decided to go to the gym. I would pant and sweat through memories of my life with Jack, from the time he approached me on campus until the day he lay next to me motionless, his spirit having departed while I slept.

The gym had become a friend of sorts, as I navigated the hellish loneliness of becoming a widow. I hadn't befriended the stiff people of Sailfish Cove. I preferred the gate guards to the residents, something Jack and I had in common. A stab of fear went through me that Officer Williams would deduce that Melissa was Jack's child and share it with the other guards. My fear was reduced when I realized Doris Williams, the gate guard, was not a gossip, and even if she were, nothing in life would alter the fact that Jack was gone.

When I arrived home from the gym, I felt a little lighter and decided to call my friend Julie. I checked the time as it was three hours earlier in L.A. Julie loved her home and still had a few teenagers whom she worshipped at home with her. Our friendship became strained when she was pregnant with her first child, Travis. Always empathetic, she waited to tell me her good news knowing the envy and angst it would invoke in me. I remember the evening she called when phone calls still arrived through land lines. I did the best I could to fake a joy I didn't feel.

But as soon as I met her little boy, nearly a toddler, hiding behind his mother's leg, I fell in love and developed a relationship with him that has lasted. Of all the sympathy notes I received after Jack's death, the one from Travis really got to me. Even if Julie prodded him to write it, the words were heartfelt and belonged to Travis, and I felt not envy of Julie's motherhood…just a strong love for her child.

I sent Julie a text before calling her. I used my land line to ensure good reception and spilled the story of meeting Melissa.

"Kathy, I've never lied to you, and I won't now. I'm truly shocked by this. Jack loved you completely. It had to be a one night thing, a blunder, an aberration."

And then she started to cry. She switched gears quickly, and in the language of best friends said between hiccups, "What's she like?"

"Sweet, young, slender…open. And she does the lip thing like Jack."

Julie became really quiet. I could tell she was about to say something I wouldn't like.

"Spit it out!" I said.

"Maybe Jack sent her to you to tell you what he died feeling guilty about. Or to keep him close to you in some way."

"Oh, for heaven sakes, Julie. Jack cheated on me. Had a child with another woman. Deceived me until the end of his life. Please don't give me your L.A. hocus-pocus.

"I'm sorry, Kathy. I really am. "

"Me too, Jules. Thanks for listening. I'm gonna go now."

The morning after my conversation with Julie, I awakened with something other than the leaden feeling of loss. I was curious. Before I lost my nerve, I sent Melissa a text and asked if she could meet me at the campus Starbucks. Although we didn't discuss much about her life, I knew she was attending Cutler University near my home. The whole encounter was so shocking, I hadn't even thought about how weird it was that she would be going to school near me.

I had a hard time holding on to anger at Jack. Or my curiosity was greater than any feeling I had felt other than grief in a long time.

Melissa stood up as soon as I entered Starbucks. She had chosen one of the cushy love seats for our meeting. It was hard not to be taken with her delicate bone structure and her open manner.

She started first. "My Mom was in remission from MS. She had a one night fling with a businessman. Not long before the MS killed her, she told me how my father loved you and made my mother feel somewhat shabby as he spoke aloud of betraying you. She told me who he was, but she never told him about me."

"Did she have a way of reaching him?" I said, stricken with fear of the other woman.

"It didn't take research to know about the Slater office, so I assume he told her that," Melissa said looking down.

"How did you meet him?"

"I interned at Slater so I could get to know him. "

"Did your mother know?"

"She was already gone when I met your husband."

My husband Jack. Gone from this world leaving me to face this alone.

Sitting here in Starbucks with Melissa Hobart Palmer. My husband's daughter.

I had no financial worries, which is a lot more than many women go through at the loss of their husbands.

"Try not to hate my Mom. She was single. She was sick. And she was happy to have me. And I, her," she said with such grace and dignity that all I could do was stare.

Melissa was well-spoken and intelligent.

She checked her phone and said she had to make a class.

We both haltingly said we would meet again, and she added a guileless, "I don't have many friends here." Neither do I, I thought to myself as I made my way home.

The following week, at Starbucks, I heard a lot more about Jack which redeemed him somewhat in my eyes.

"When I got up the nerve to meet with Mr. Palmer privately, he belittled me by expressing regret, then saw I felt hurt, and softened his tone. He knew the encounter that caused me to be in the world, and he lost all veneer of Mr. Businessman, and told me about you, and how he had to live with the guilt of that night in Chicago."

Oh Jack, I hope you suffered, I thought as I was dying for more details of the part that made me seem cherished. I didn't want the part where Melissa's mother had six pack abs, or something like that.

On a subsequent trip to Starbucks, Melissa was free from classes, and I invited her to my home for take-out food. We settled on Chinese. I couldn't ask Melissa all the questions I wanted to about her mother, as the young woman was clearly grief-stricken without her. I knew the feeling. During the Chinese meal which allowed us to loosen up, she told me how she and Cutler University came together.

Jack, who only met Melissa in the past year, pre-paid her tuition in a gesture to bring her close to us.

"We had a few lunches in a deli, where he was guarded, and told me about you....a lot. He said after you killed him, you would be decent to me. I believed him, so here I am. And you are better than decent."

Did I kill Jack? I wondered...all that passive aggression, and obsession over our lack of children? Harping on him that he worked too much, which allowed me to sit here in a beautiful home paid for...no mortgage note strangling me...

I began to enjoy meeting Melissa, better than my outings with some of my neighbors.

One evening, three months after meeting her, I admitted to myself that I liked Jack's kid. . Perhaps it was aided by the chardonnay I was sipping.

We agreed that she would call Jack just that... Jack.

"Jack didn't take care of living expenses. Don't get me wrong. I'm grateful as hell to be at Cutler. But I probably won't be able to stay on, without a better job," she said matter-of- factly.

This was the same night I asked if Jack wanted a paternity test.

"No he knew my mother's name, and that she lived in Naperville."

I had a hard time breathing thinking of his remembering this woman's name for twenty years. I nearly lost all kindly feelings about the situation.

But as I was walking Melissa to her car, I imagined hearing the cuckoo clock Jack was so fond of ticking in the den, and I was hit with such a stab of loneliness I said,

"There's plenty of room for you here in your father's home, Melissa."

She did the lip thing, and looked away and said quietly, "Thanks Mrs. Palmer."

"Kathy," I said, blinking back tears. "Please call me Kathy."

From: Adelaide Magazine

A MOVING TARGET

Amy drug the wooden chair across the porch. "How many times are you going to scrape the floor?" I asked her, slightly annoyed.

"I want to get a better look at the road. And we're just renting the place, Julie. Sip your drink, and leave me alone."

I had fallen in love with the beach cottage we had chosen for our reunion, and felt hurt when Amy dissed it. Amy and I were roommates, but some of us hadn't been together since college. It had only been five years, but in the emotional turmoil of twenty-somethings, it felt like a very long time.

" I hear she got married recently," Amy perked up and pulled her chair closer to mine. Both of us wanted to spot Isabel the moment she arrived.

The cottage was directly across from the ocean, close enough to see the sand pipers scurrying at water's edge. Amy and I were on a mission. We were going to rectify our shabby treatment of Isabel.

When Isabel accepted in an e-mail, I sent Amy a text.

"Did you see who accepted?"

"Some of us work, Julie" was the response. I knew Amy had seen it. She checked her e-mail like a maniac, and her tart response proved it.

It all started with a dare.

Isabel had been a bit of an outcast. Introverted and extremely intelligent, she became an enigma for her house mates in the home we shared during school. Amy and I were already friends when we set up our living quarters, newly emancipated from the stifling dorm. Isabel arrived at our front door holding one of the notes we attached to a cork board on campus.

Amy and I needed the rent money and would have accepted just about anybody.

I was going through a mean stage when I opened the door to a geeky girl with glasses.

She was fodder for the evil that coursed through me, reeling from my break-up with John. She held up our note advertising for roomies, and I invited her in. Amy and I promised we would jointly agree on whom we accepted. Just when I began to fret, Amy arrived from her job at the campus book store.

Gesturing in the language of good friends, I pointed upstairs where Isabel was checking out the place.

"She's kind of geeky," I whispered. "But not scary or anything."

"You didn't accept her without me, did you?"

"No, Ms. Bossy. Go upstairs and introduce yourself," I told Amy, who was already en route. I eavesdropped as best I could, picking up tone and nuance. Amy liked Isabel just fine. And that's how it started.

"I forget what the rent is," Isabel said resting after her tour, sipping Amy's green tea.

"How can she not know the amount? " I hissed to Amy when Isabel went back upstairs to check out her room.

"Didn't you hear her say her parents are paying?"

A hot fury arose in me, never far buried in the dregs of my break-up. She's obviously smart and rich, I thought, looking for a target. I was not too thrilled with Amy's dopey smile, spiffing up the living room, either.

The other room, as we later named it, was a revolving cast of characters, some of whom were joining us for the reunion.

I jumped when Amy snapped her fingers in front of my face.

"I still could kill John for what he did to you, Julie."

"The worst part was my being mean to Isabel, " I said, regretting how quickly I admitted it. Amy played a part in the set-up too. After Isabel was comfortably settled in, we learned she had a huge crush on Matt Miller, one of the hottest guys on campus. It bothered me that she felt she could arouse his interest with her unkempt, nerdy looks. I had a pick on her from the start.

Amy topped off my wine and we relaxed on the porch of our cottage.

" They should have named our place zoo central," she said pointing to a white bird.

"Lucky we weren't busted with some of those parties," I said remembering the scent of weed and beer, stragglers asleep on the living room floor.

Maybe the wine was getting to me, but I wanted to blame Amy for setting up Isabel.

" You didn't kill anybody, Julie," she said, when I started to re-play the incident.

" It was an off time for you. Not that big of a deal. Forgive yourself, but don't blame me."

"You suggested the note from my brother with guy's handwriting."

"Julie, that was just an offhand statement. You were more than happy to run with it."

And run with it I did. I told my brother I needed certain words written in a guy's handwriting. I caught him when he was distracted and mumbled something about a writing class. I told him what to write and asked him to sign it Matt.

"What's it for?" he asked pen aloft.

"We're studying differences in men and women's writing. Part of a puff course."

I knew asking him to do the envelope was too much so Amy asked her boyfriend to do it. He would have flown to the moon on a scooter for her, on a bad day.

Isabel was on her way to a class when I pointed to the envelope on top of our mail table in the hall.

"It was put through our mail slot," I told her as I brushed by her, veering right behind her to our living room. She placed it inside her old-fashioned school bag and said "See ya Julie," as she gently closed the front door.

Did I imagine the wistful look as she slid her glasses to her head when she read her name? Or had the seeds of guilt harassed my vision?

I needed to keep the message simple or my brother wouldn't have gone along.

"I've noticed."

"Matt."

I insisted my brother leave enough room for me to put in something else between the comment and the signature. Amy and I agreed it had a compelling romantic allure as it was. Simple, yet mysterious.

Seated comfortably on the porch with Amy, I allowed myself to re-live the moment Isabel curled up to Matt Miller, tipsy and confident, and his attempts to untangle himself from her, our couch, and our party.

It was Amy who heard him say kindly. "Isabel, I never sent you a note."

"You're starting to obsess, Jules," Amy said, as I shook my head letting the salt air tickle my nose.

"I heard Karen Turner works with a trainer, and looks like Rambo," I said, forcing myself back into the present.

"I've seen her posts on Facebook," Amy said. "She changed her status to single recently. She and her boyfriend were together forever. I wonder what happened."

"We'll know soon enough," I said walking my wine glass into the kitchen.

"Let's walk the beach. We don't own the place, as you mentioned. We can leave a sticky note on the door."

I let whoever arrived first know Amy and I were walking the beach. I requested a text upon arrival. I had stuck an extra key under a jagged rock near the porch, but chose not to advertise that on the note.

" Isabel asked for my contact info and sent me a text," Amy said when we descended the short wooden staircase to the beach. The sand was fine and soothing to my feet. It had been a while since I felt that soft cushion.

While leaning down to roll up her jeans, Amy said, " Isabel said her husband may drop her off at the cottage. "

" Ironic that she's the only one of us married. I'm not much on Facebook and haven't kept up with everybody, so I'm not sure," I said, as we picked up our pace at water's edge.

"We know Karen is single, and I'm not sure about some of the others," Amy said.

"Now you're making me paranoid that somebody turned into a crack addict or something," Amy added. "We pulled this reunion together quickly. "

"It will be fine," I said, surprising myself with my sunny outlook.

Much of Amy's friendship with me was akin to a jail term, with my inability to move on past John. I had hook-ups, but nothing serious since that time outside my dorm when he pulled up the hood on my rain jacket, and told me he needed space.

I'm still humiliated how badly I crumbled in front of him, my disappointment rendering me helpless. His rejection tapped into my worst fears that I was unlovable, lacking in something basic. I had visions of the perfect woman for John, and hoped he had not met her yet.

The visions changed from the clean-cut preppy look, to the physics prof with glasses. And we all know what happens when the glasses get shed. I hated all of them, these imagined women, able to earn John's love, while I was left with space, acres and acres of empty space.

My reverie was broken by the slight buzz in my pocket - a text from Karen Turner that she was on the porch waiting for us.

Amy and I hosed off our sandy feet and hurried back to the cottage.

"Don't forget to compliment her strong physique," I said, as we crossed the street.

" And let's avoid any questions about her ex," Amy added.

Karen looked spectacular...and happy.

"You guys look great, too" she said, as she entered the kitchen rolling her suitcase.

"The De Angelo twins were right behind me on the road," Karen said, as she plopped down onto the couch.

"Those guys were the best people in the other room," Amy said.

"Oh, for heaven's sakes, Amy. They were slobs. Stoned all the time, and cleaning us out with the munchies," I said.

"But for guys, they were good about re-stocking the fridge. And they paid the rent on time," Amy said.

A renewed flash of envy shot through me thinking of Isabel's parents paying a year in advance.

After Karen settled into her room, she joined Amy and me on the porch.

It wasn't long until we heard the rumble of the twins' F 150.

Although fraternal twins, the De Angelo brothers looked nearly identical. Tony, rounded the truck with a "Yo," and Karen stood up and waved.

After a few awkward moments, we were fairly comfortable with them even though they both looked more attractive than I remembered.

Amy shot me a look while standing up straighter, fingers stroking back her hair.

She saw it too. The twins looked great.

Although we didn't know Karen too well, I saw tightening of her biceps and a good deal of cleavage as we settled into the living room.

Always good at providing for themselves, the De Angelos brought a cooler of beer brimming with ice.

We started naming the inhabitants of the other room, several of whom were joining us.

"Let's not get plastered," I said. "We're grown-ups now."

Amy shot me a look that proved to me she was into Nick De Angelo.

" Not that we get plastered a lot..." I added lamely, not wanting to deter Nick from Amy.

More friends arrived. Some brought guests, and there were a few coin flips for the pull-out couches and futons. I gave up hope for an organized reunion, and felt a flush of whimsy. But my natural sense of order did check the ice maker, and filled a few ice cube trays for back-up. I didn't want to be stuck with the ice from the twins' beer cooler.

While stirring the ice in the freezer bucket, I heard a weird tone to Amy's voice as she said, "Here comes Isabel." I froze in place.

Although it never fully surfaced that I was the perp in the note fiasco, Isabel knew. I could feel her long looks at me when my back was turned stirring a pot of chili, or cleaning out the fridge. Her gracefulness blossomed under our roof, knowing perhaps, that she was on her own.

My meanness backfired on me, as is so often the case...

There were jovial greetings in the living room; the evening becoming a party.

I felt him before I saw him.

"Julie. How have you been?"

I'd know that voice forever.

Even after all this time, his physical presence rocked me. I leaned against the stove and said, "John, we didn't expect you."

"I'm not staying. I'm dropping off my wife."

The word wife sliced through me. My spy network had scattered post college, and I knew John wouldn't go for social media.

" We're newlyweds," he beamed, and caught himself.

Had I become so neutral in his affection that he forgot how I might take that?

I struggled to speak, trying to say congratulations.

I couldn't.

They best I could do was to ask where they had met.

" I met Isabel in the lab in grad school."

In the midst of my shock, I thought of the physics prof with glasses, the fictional target of my ire. Isabel. John married Isabel. The enormity of it. The irony. Or was it?

" John, did you know we were house mates?"

" I don't know," he said, as he darted his eyes. His protecting her hit me as strongly as his marriage.

" John, you need to get going," Isabel said as she circled his waist with her arm.

" Hi Julie. You look good," she said. Glowing. Triumphant. The nerd telling the cool girl to stick it.The nerd with the only man I ever loved. Normal. Fitting in. Married.

Amy skidded around the corner to rescue me, her loyalty as big as her heart.

Seeing my trusted friend and John in the same room, I began to open a bit to this shocking news.

"Best wishes to you both!" I said, not quite meaning it, but feeling as if I were emerging from a cave into the light.

My limbs felt heavy with loss, and yet I felt a sliver of hope.

I still loved John. Probably always would, But it was time to get among the living.

Time to stretch and sway with growth.

Take that dance class.

Learn to speak French.

Give Amy the friendship she deserved.

Open my heart again.

While I turned back to the fridge, Amy tapped my shoulder. Alone in the kitchen, we hugged each other fiercely.

" That was tough stuff," she said.

I squeezed her a bit longer.

Tony De Angelo peeked into the kitchen and said, " You two are missing the party."

So we joined our friends, who were laughing and swaying to the soft music, it's tone above a whisper, but enough for us to join in the dance.

From: Foliate Oak Literary Magazine

THE BALDWIN INN

" Miss Hill, Mr. Baldwin and I thought you forgot all about us"
Mrs. B said in the foyer of their restaurant, as Miss Hill shyly
adjusted her shawl. " We want you to sit near the fireplace, your
favorite spot." Mrs. Baldwin never missed an opportunity to
welcome an elderly visitor. I worked there during college, and
can still hear the clatter in the kitchen; the chefs chopping onions,
and the waitresses venting about ornery customers.

    Although the owner enjoyed greeting guests with his wife, he
was often called upon
to fill in for a missing chef or two. The Baldwin Inn was a rustic
spot near Philly which catered to a gentle, refined crowd. Many of
the guests had been widowed, or never married, and the gentlemen
parked their hats in the coat room, adjacent to the foyer. The
ambiance spoke of manners and traditions lost to my generation,
with our keg parties and blaring music.

    The plush chairs along the walls provided the clientele with
comfortable support during the waiting period.

    As I reflected upon my service at The Baldwin Inn, I often felt a
spark of joy. The elderly patrons barely concealed their delight to
be so warmly embraced by the owners. The Baldwins' kindness
relieved me of the drudgery of the work itself. I felt their ads
should say " Send your mother and grandmother here. They will be
treated like family."

The elder Baldwin son, Douglas, stopped in regularly, sometimes with his charming wife Sandra, and one of their feisty daughters.

Steven, the younger son, evoked a searing pain in the Baldwins, especially Mrs. B. Although New York was not a great distance, Steven still remained a pained absence in the window seats of the Inn. Muffled rumors floated through the noisy kitchen and the muted foyer. Sorting through the whispers, I concluded that the feud was between the brothers, but Steven blamed his parents. A familiar story to so many.....

My own sons, both in college, shone brighter in the company of the other. Gratitude swelled within me as I lay aside the letter from Douglas Baldwin. My kids were friends. Fearing sad news, I needed a few moments to remember that time in my life, before I read the message.

The bus I had taken to New York to visit my friend Mona reeked of stale smoke and alcohol.
Her friends invited me to a surprise party in Greenwich Village. Her twenty- first birthday, two months before my own, promised a zany assortment of actors. Most paid for their tiny quarters doing the same work as I. Few admitted that.

Before embarking upon my New York trip, I snuck into the office at the Inn to sneak a look at Steven's New York address. Mona knew the street as it intersected her favorite coffee shop.

Delighted, and completely surprised, Mona floated through her party with the flair of a blossoming artist.

The weekend opened in me a sliver of risk taking. Did it take courage to creep up the staircase of Steven Baldwin's brownstone? Perhaps. But I think it was more likely the exuberance of youth. His hostility cloaked him like a spider's web. He wouldn't let me into his place, but, then again, I was a stranger. It struck me that I needed to get to the point quickly. He pushed aside the worn looking, wobbly table near him, and opened the door an inch. His face softened slightly when I spoke of his mother. I remember faded rust on his front door as it closed.

Seated comfortably in my den, my husband out golfing, I opened the letter from Douglas. My tongue felt heavy as I read about the loss of his mother. The service would be followed by a reception at The Baldwin Inn. Douglas added a heartfelt personal note to me. The family would be honored if I could join them. My husband Alex returned from his outing so elated about his putting, I could have suggested a trip to Mars and he would endorse it. " She meant a lot to you, Cassie. Go to the service." He said gently.

Sandra Baldwin greeted me in the entrance of the funeral service. Her daughters, now grown women, surrounded their father like sentries. "Cassie, it's so good to see you again," Sandra said warmly. " You helped bring Steven back home." Another guest drew her attention away from me as I walked through the dimly lit hallway to Douglas.

He hugged me, saying my name softly. " I loved your mother, Douglas. I am very sorry."

Mingling with the other mourners, I learned that Steven returned home often, before the cancer prevented his seeing age thirty-five. I overheard that Douglas held Steven's gaunt body closely at the end.

Under the place card which stated my name, there was a note from Douglas. " Thank you, Cassie. If you wish to add to the tributes to mother, please do. "

During a loll in the tributes, I stood up and raised my glass. " I worked here for the Baldwins during college. Mrs. Baldwin treated her customers like family. She gave elderly guests the courage to dine alone. 'Mrs. Parker, does your daughter still live in D.C.?' 'Mr. Williams, we have wild salmon this evening.' Her kindness expressed her faith in action. So let's toast Mrs. Baldwin and enjoy this meal in her honor. I trust that many elder souls are preparing her a celestial meal."

From: Potluck Magazine

ABOUT THE AUTHOR

Edith Gallagher Boyd is a graduate of Temple University. a former French teacher, and an avid sports fan. She and her family live in Jupiter, Florida.

Made in the USA
Middletown, DE
19 February 2019